FOR

THE

LOVE

OF

LEE

FOR
THE
LOVE
OF
LEE

Jennifer Janell

CONTENTS

ACKNOWLEDGEMENTS

I would like to thank my family for supporting me while writing this book. I know it wasn't easy, but it was worth it. Special thanks to Khloe's Thoughts Editing Services for editing, and Monique Mensah for coaching me and getting this book into readers' hands. I couldn't have done it without all of you.

DEDICATION

This book is dedicated to all of us who strive to accept the imperfections in ourselves and others. May we realize that it just doesn't matter…

-Jennifer Janell

PROLOGUE

The belief that I was a useless burden was introduced by my father. His cruel words forced me on an inevitable path to find purpose and belonging. As I matured, the hunt for purpose morphed into the need for power and control. Between my thighs I found the irresistible treasure, a power that was never useless or worthless. It wouldn't help me find true love, but love was the last thing I wanted. Love and attachments were just a means to great disappointments and pain. My past relationships consisted of lying, cheating, and meaningless sex, but securing the company of men remained my secret challenge for validation.

The avoidance of a committed, healthy relationship propelled me into the direction of the toxic ones, which had a destructive impact on my life. Perceptions, people, and their expectations coaxed me into reckless situations at the expense of my morality. The bonds I formed were refined or ruined, based on my perception of what relationships should be. I could easily say my mind played the cruelest, reality altering jokes.

It was time for a change. I had to break free from toxic relationships, reconcile with my past, and work toward a life that would benefit me. I set my self-improvement plans in motion, but the universe had so much more in store for me.

CHAPTER 1

Self-Control

Mike was begging me to open the door. I've been seeing him for a while, but he was never meant for me to keep. Mike was a married man and now he was here, attempting to hold on to a relationship I never should've started.

"Leesha, please open the door. Let me talk to you."

His knocking was relentless. Any other day, I would've opened it, told him it was over, then he would fuck me crazy, making me a fool over another woman's man, yet again. The promise to let go of self-destructive things was a long time coming for me. Mike's dick was definitely a ride at your own risk, self-destructive trip. But now it was time for me to love myself, whatever that meant. I was trying to figure out what self-love looked like.

The last year had been a whirlwind of solicited and unsolicited encounters, friendships, and bonds. It had been a good year made by terrible decisions. Last year was my "why not? You only live once, what's the worst that could happen?" year. Now, the answer to that reckless question was knocking at my door.

I paced back and forth wringing my hands, confused about letting him in. Anger, sadness, and guilt clouded my judgement. I was laying in the bed I made. My mother always said, if I made my bed hard, I had to lay in it. Actually, the bed is what got me into this mess.

The banging was becoming more aggressive when I heard my neighbor's door open.

"Hey man, do you mind? It's obvious she isn't home and I'm trying to get some work done." Johnathon's voice was intimidating. There was silence after the door slammed.

"Thank you, Lord," I whispered and tiptoed to the peephole to scope out the hallway. No one was there. I ran to my balcony to see Mike walking to his car and watched as he turned onto the access road. The San Antonio heat made me quickly retreat into my cool apartment. It was hard being such a bitch, but it was for my greater good, I'd blocked my blessings for too long. I laid down on the couch, comforted by the cool, soft leather and the aroma of lavender room spray, and drifted off to sleep.

The smell of food creeping through the walls woke me a few hours later. Johnathon was cooking, so I decided to invite myself over. I threw on some cut-off denim shorts and an oversized t-shirt. My beer caddy was ready in the fridge filled with six beers, and I added a bottle of chilled Stella Rosa to contribute to the meal. Johnathon was always ready for drinks, hopefully beer and wine was enough. I took a deep breath, prepared for the upcoming conversation, and headed next door.

As my door shut, Johnathon's opened. "I was wondering when your greedy ass was going to smell these pork chops! Come in." Johnathon eyed me from head to toe. I could tell he had already been drinking and was going to be more feminine than masculine tonight. He was bisexual, so it was like having a good girlfriend with a great male's point of view. He also was a fabulous cook, and the apartment smelled like heaven.

"I brought beer and wine. Which one do you want tonight?"

"Both! Damn, I knew about those two dudes, but their persistence is crazy. Yea, we need beer and the wine tonight!" He rolled his golden-brown eyes obviously annoyed with me. Johnathon stood 6'3" and had smooth, honey-brown skin. His perfect lips highlighted those sparkly white teeth when he smiled. It's no wonder men liked him just as much as women did. Who could resist those long eyelashes? Right now, I just wanted to avoid those eyes. He was my best friend, but he could be *judgy* sometimes.

"Johnathon, you know the deal with that. We discussed it, and I'm doing surprisingly well. I'm not letting any of them enter my home, destroy my peace, or block my blessings. I promised not to mess with them anymore. It's time to just do my own thing and the next man I let in, will be someone I love and is available to just me." Convincing myself was probably harder than convincing him.

"Yea, yea keep telling yourself that. That dude Mike gonna come by sweet talking and swinging that dick around, then there you go. Anyway, what if one of your *casuals* decides to try to kick my ass for shooing him away?" This time, he was the one that couldn't maintain eye contact. He was more than just bothered about this.

"Well, us big girls are hard to resist." I slowly swayed my hips back and forth, hoping to ease the tension Johnathon was stirring up. I wasn't uncomfortably big, but I had some thick ass thighs, slightly smaller waist, and large breasts. "Thank you for having my back on this." I was grateful for his support, regardless of how he felt about it. Johnathon thought he knew everything about me, but he found out that wasn't the case. Self-control didn't come easy for me; it was as if I depended on men to fulfill my empty spaces.

Dinner was great. We drank two beers each, the bottle of wine, then took a couple of shots, which kept us laughing for the rest of the night. He brought out some weed, and surely, he had it laced with something because I damn near blacked out every time we smoked it. But I never asked because ignorance was bliss.

Johnathon opened up about this guy at work he was crushing on. He was always very professional there, so he avoided shameless flirting. If you didn't know Johnathon, you would think he was straight with just microscopic hints of femininity. The fact that he slipped up and had a threesome with some female coworkers after last year's Christmas party didn't help either.

"Johnathon, the only way you could possibly have a chance with this guy is to be honest, but discreet. Tell him you do not want to offend him but ask if he is open to dating men. If he says yes and is available, ask him out." I was always ready to give relationship advice, but not the best to be in one. Yes, I was that friend.

Before the night was over, Johnathon promised to talk to the guy at work, and I promised to stay on my self-love journey. It was 2 a.m. when I stumbled back to my place. *I really should stop doing that shit with him,* I thought.

I woke up at about 10:30 that morning. Johnathon was playing music, and his vacuum was running. *Where does he get all this energy from?* Anyway, it was my day to rest and relax. Tomorrow was a workday, and a wealthy family was supposed to visit Lotus Gardens this week. They were looking at facilities for their grandmother. They didn't care to give an exact date and time, which I considered to be rude. It was voluntold to me by the owner to do the tour for the family. I was making it a point to look extra nice every day.

I reflected on my night with Johnathon. Damn, I smoked that shit, ate all the food that was not allowed on my diet, and drank way too much. Talking about my past and getting all sentimental was another mistake. All of that should've been avoided. *Fuck, I have no self-control. Well, today is a new day, and a little self-care is another start over.*

After completing my Sunday's routine of washing my hair, shaving, and preparing for the upcoming week, I examined myself in the mirror. The carb-reducing diet was working, and the new hair products made my hair thick and shiny. I placed some whitening strips on my teeth, thanking Mom for getting me braces in high school. My curves looked more like lumps now. The confidence and admiration immediately turned into insecurity. At least I had good skin. My caramel breasts were firm and decorated with big Hershey's Kisses that made any dick stand at attention. A delicately designed tattooed cross graced my left thigh with vibrant vines of roses traveling up my back around to my right shoulder. After the false-hearted reassurance that I looked okay after the night of indulgence, I slipped my robe on with a vow to do better. Little did I know, my life would unexpectedly look different in a year.

CHAPTER 2

Something to Prove

I t had been two weeks, and I was doing great with my much-needed solitary self-reformation. There was no frantic knocking at my door, less smoking, drinking, and eating. I spent more time working out and renewing friendships. I impressed myself when I laid in my bed before 11 p.m. on that Sunday night, which was a good time compared to the normal after midnight bedtime. In an attempt to fall asleep, my mind wandered, and Mike Adams' face popped into my head.

I met him at my regular coffee spot. Damn, he was so fine. The fact he was married made him easy to let go. God only knew why I fooled around with him. Maybe it was his dark skin, beautiful dark eyes, and those mesmerizing lips. When he spoke, all I could look at was that black, perfectly groomed mustache and beard. He always smelled delicious.

Mike chased me until I finally agreed to one drink at my place. It was downhill from there. His 6'2" body towered over me. Once he finally cornered me and gave me a kiss, I damn near blacked out. Matter of fact, I think I did. Next thing I knew, he had my legs off the ground and around his waist. My mind raced, convincing myself that this was a one-time thing. Shit, no one had to know, and he surely wouldn't speak of this night with the risk of his wife finding out.

He carried me to bed, laid me down, stood up, and slowly removed his clothes. It was like he wanted me to study every inch of him and remember that African God that stood before me. His body was breathtaking. He slowly undressed me and was steady and deliberate with every move, followed by soft, sensual kisses. He didn't kiss the cat, but she damn sure meowed for him. Mike was obviously a breasts man. He opened his mouth wide, letting my breasts slide in. His tongue circled and lapped at my nipples as his thick finger slid in and out of my pussy, causing a creamy downpour. After sliding a condom on and positioning my legs over his shoulders, he began to glide in and out of my pussy. His muscles flexed as he shifted me into different po-sitions, working out my body. The dick was so fucking per-fect. That was the only way to describe it. His strokes were rhythmic, long, and powerful, and he had me cumming all night. This could only happen once; it was way too good.

He became one of my regular lovers. Yes, lovers; he wasn't the lone ranger in my book. But each time he fucked me like he was the one and only. Each time he fucked me like he had something to prove.

If he wasn't married, we would be perfect, but it probably would've had been a competition on who was going to cheat first. I would've had a problem trusting him because the dick was so damn good. I decided to just keep seeing him, but not get too crazy. My number two helped me with that. His competition was a tough act to follow. That was the year it was going to be all about selfish little me, and I wasn't going to be played. I was the master of this game now, and it felt good, like I was finally in control of something. I didn't feel too bad about him being married, especially if he didn't eat pussy. Surely his wife of fifteen years found someone else to do that for her. I mean, who could live without that? Who would want to? Not me.

Mike caused me a lot of heartache, too. Aside from being a cheater, he was like the male version of me. We liked the same music, cars, food, and temperature in the house and car. Okay, the temperature thing sounded petty, but that was a pet peeve of mine. I hated being too hot or too cold. He was a partner at an up-and-coming law firm and told me entertaining stories about his clients. There were many nights I lit the good candles, and we listened to 90s R&B, drank brown liquor, and talked for hours. He was the one to call when I just wanted to chill. He was never pushy or acted entitled to sex. He spoke about his marriage but never said anything bad about his wife. I asked several times, "Why are you here?" One night, he finally gave me an answer.

"Because I saw you and I just wanted to know you. Not that I don't love my wife, or plan to leave her, but you sparked my curiosity. I wanted something different so, I thought it would be fun to playfully pursue you. I never in a million years thought you would oblige me, and say come over. Unfortunately, I got here and became a horny teenager. Now I don't want to leave you alone." He was arrogant and nonchalant.

"So, are you asking me to stay here and be your side piece?" I felt insulted, but I knew I was in too deep to contemplate leaving him alone.

"I guess that's what I am saying, and I feel like shit about it." He was brutally honest.

"What if I call your wife?" I wondered if he felt like shit, but I doubted it.

"Not your style."

"How do you know?"

"I know."

His confidence almost made me sick. I thought of him differently after that conversation. His cocky and conceited attitude costed him the small space he held in my heart, but it didn't stop me from seeing him. I played my position accordingly and didn't cause him any trouble, only because I liked his company, and was still infatuated with the smell and taste of his lips when he drank whisky. Getting drunk with him was dangerous, filled with addictive sex and uncontrollable feelings. He never let me down, always proving why he deserved to be in my presence. Every time I would vow to leave him alone, but that 'just one more time' turned into another and another.

One night, his wife called while he was at my place. He didn't answer, but she called back-to-back.

"Hey, Trish, baby, what's up?"

I couldn't make out all her words, but she was pissed. The conversation continued with him dodging her questions.

"I am working late; yes, again. You're acting crazy. I ain't doing shit but working. I'm tired of this insecure psycho shit, you always think I got something going on. I love you! What the fuck do I need to cheat on you for?" Mike was a fucking snake.

Jealousy began to creep up. There was no reason for me to feel that way, but those damn feelings took control. As he was talking, I walked to the foot of the bed, looked him in the eyes, and dropped my robe, revealing my naked body. His body shivered then he grabbed his dick, trying to keep it down. His wife's emotional voice didn't stop me from vying for his attention. I sat on the bed facing him, legs wide open, playing with myself while he lied to his wife and watched me. He reached for me, and I slapped his hand.

"Don't fucking touch me," I whispered. He threw his hand up in frustration, and his dick was at full attention now.

"Trish, let me finish up. I'll be home in a minute." He hung the phone up. I got up, tied my robe, and went into the restroom, slamming the door.

"What the fuck is going on here! Why are you tripping now!" Mike was yelling. He hit the bathroom door, and I slung it open.

"Go home to Trish!"

"Why the fuck you mad, Lee? You knew I was married; you knew what this was. Now you fucking around, playing with your pussy and shit, telling me don't touch you? Like I been keeping secrets from you! Help me understand this shit!"

"Yea, Michael, you right, I knew what this was, maybe I can't deal with this shit; sitting around and hearing you say you love her right after you just screwed me! Just go home, Michael, I need to think about how you need to be handled." He had already dressed and was walking out the door.

That entire scene was eye opening. Selfish, pitiful, desperate, and crazy couldn't began to describe the way I was acting. You would think I was the one with something to prove. So, when I let him go in an effort to make space for myself and the right person, I literally went through withdrawals, wanting to call him, see him, and feel him; knowing there was no benefit. Sending him straight to voicemail and not opening the door when he showed up was my way of taking control back from him. The thing was, I never told him I was done, part of me wanted to be able to pick him back up in case weakness set in and my body required his attention. Not making our break-up clear to him left that door cracked.

CHAPTER 3

Unexpected Lesson

Like I said, there were a few others to keep me occupied when Mike wasn't around, but only one was worth mentioning. I met Roy Walker when I was jogging in the park. My size never stopped me from working out with the best of them. He was looking at me for some days before finally speaking. His braces made his twenty-six years look more like eighteen. I looked young for my thirty-one years but was always a little self-conscious when we went out. Roy was light skinned with hazel eyes, tall, lean, and muscular. He wore his hair in a tight fade and had strong facial features, with a prominent nose and charming smile. He was the fun one, and that was what I needed. We would go to the movies, basketball games, and eat on the Riverwalk. No sex, just laughing, talking, and flirting. I felt like a high school girl dating the star basketball player.

One night, we were hanging out at my place, and he kissed me. This kiss wasn't like the previous ones, it was lengthy and passionate. He looked hesitant to go too far, so I was the one to take charge, straddled him, and took off his shirt. He took the hint, pulled down my oversized shirt, and unhooked my bra. His eyes glimmered as my breasts fell, grazing his lips prompting him to taste them. His lips and tongue encouraged my next move. I stood up, took his hand, and led him to my room.

As soon as the door closed, Roy let me know he was the one in control now. His kiss was aggressive, and his tongue made me melt by the second, instantly dampening my panties. My body moved with Roy's to the bed and the thick, pink comforter cushioned my soft fall. He quickly undressed me, and anxiety filled my body as he kneeled and pulled me to the edge of the bed. Roy slowed down and began kissing and licking my inner thighs. His tongue traced up to my pussy, then eased into a long, slow lick that lingered at my opening, resting on my clit. The warm air from his mouth as he slowly licked and kissed took my pussy to glory. My quiet moans became gasps as I came, feeling my nectar trickle down my ass. He made sure I was polished clean before standing up.

"Scoot back," he ordered.

I slid my body to the middle of the bed, and he took off his sweatpants and laid between my legs, lifting them up. Roy's dick was long, thick, with a slight right curve. There was no hesitation when he entered me and proceeded with strong steady strokes. He was holding back, so I grabbed his face and gave him a lustful, tongue filled kiss, letting him know this girl wanted … no, needed to be fucked. He grabbed my thighs harder, and his strokes deepened with increased speed. After a good amount of mind-blowing fucking, his hand slapped and firmly gripped my thigh, signaling for me to turn over. I flipped to all fours, lifting my ass for his visual pleasure.

"Oh fuck," Roy groaned in appreciation as he slid back into me. He worked me until we both came. Damn he was so sexy; Roy didn't make love, straight fucking was his style, and it was good. From then on, he had me and he knew it.

Roy and I could've been a great couple, but I refused to get too close, and thought he was too young and fine for me. That was a dangerous combination. Unfortunately, jealousy was an issue for me, so I limited intimate moments with him because dating was better. I enjoyed getting dressed and looking pretty. We were both the type that demanded attention when we walked into a room. The men sneaking a smile or giving me the once over behind his back made me feel good. Surely the ladies were doing the same to him; if they only knew how addictive he could be if not careful.

Roy kept my mind off Mike and when we slept together, he always talked about how lucky he was to have met me. He was good for the self-esteem if anything, always aiming to please, and I appreciated that.

There came a time when Roy wasn't as available. My insecurities told me that he had a new woman. What could I say, I always told him we were just "friends with benefits," but now I was feeling possessive. I called him at unusual times, hoping to get rid of this woman. I was definitely out of character and imagined this woman was younger, thinner, and prettier. He ignored my calls until one night when he finally answered.

"Lee, what is going on? Are you okay? You been calling like crazy." He'd never sounded so irritated with me.

"I was just checking on you. Did I interrupt something?" I matched his energy.

"What? You mean, am I fucking someone? Shouldn't I be asking you that, friend?"

"Okay, that's fair." That comment caught me off guard.

"Lee, I ain't trying to hurt you. But we are not serious, right?"

"Right." I shook my head and stared at the floor.

"I'm not serious with anyone, so don't trip. I'll come see you tomorrow."

"Okay."

Roy had every right to be turned off. He gave me a dose of my own medicine. He taught me how it felt to be cheated on. I was cheated on before, but this was different; it was done because I was doing it first and that cut a little deeper. And there I was again, number two, another side chick. Another hard, unexpected lesson learned.

The next day, Roy came over. He was in a good mood. The fact that he'd finally gotten my attention and made me act semi-psycho was great for him.

"Why have you been acting so needy lately? That's not your style." The half-smile on his face irritated the shit out of me.

Little did he know, "needy" was my middle name now days. "I'm good, I was missing you a little, but I understand you got things going on."

Why was I always okay with a man that had other "things" going on? My spirit was so unsettled with acting less than. Although I brought this on myself, I was done and ready to cut him off too. Seriously done being my own worst enemy, done holding on to the bad and letting the good slip through my fingers.

CHAPTER 4

Damaged Goods

Ms. Franklin was my psychologist. She always wanted to "deep dive" into every comment I made. At least that is how I saw it. She made me explain what I meant by "the mess I have made of my life." It wasn't hard to figure out; I had some issues. My father was white and from a well-known family. After he died, I promised myself to never feel helpless again. He was gone and no one could take his place of making me feel like a worthless accident. The memory of my father's death triggered my constant nightmares.

I had been seeing Ms. Franklin for six months. The first three months, she was just in my business. She would listen and made me explain every little word said or excuse I made. She eventually helped me realize my feelings were just that; mine and no one else's. So, I became painfully honest about my life, past, present, and future. She listened to my truths like it was a dramatic TV series. She was way too interested and probably needed some excitement or dysfunction of her own.

I told her of my childhood, the good and bad. The good times consisted of being with my mother before she took me to live with my father, his wife, and daughter. My mother and I abruptly left my grandmother's house in the middle of the night. I wasn't sure why; all I knew was my mother was desperate to get out of there. We ended up living in a small apartment and from what I remember, had a small Christmas tree that was lit up all the time. We ate, watched TV, and played in that one spot in the bed. There was no couch, no chairs, and no separate bedroom. It was just us two, and Mom made everything into a game. I also remember hearing her cry at night, but she would never say why.

Then one day, she picked me up from school and told me I was staying with my father for a little while. I remember crying, screaming, and telling her how I hated her. I was so angry because I had only seen my father twice and he didn't even hug me. She abandoned me. When she dropped me off, I didn't talk to her, no goodbye, just tears.

My father made it clear that he wasn't happy to have me around, tarnishing his pure white reputation. His wife, Helen, tried to make me feel welcomed, but his meanness overshadowed everything nice she tried to do. It wasn't long before Helen started mistreating me too. They usually ignored me, I wasn't allowed to eat dinner at the table, and sometimes was locked in the closet for having a 'smart mouth.'

My sister was Leanna. We were both named after my father Lee, but luckily, she was the one that got to carry the last name, Mohan. She would watch and sometimes cry for me. One time I was in the closet, and she sat by the door.

In her weak, scared voice she said, "I'm sorry, sister."

"It's okay, Leanna. Can you call my momma?"

"I don't know how." She sounded as miserable as I felt.

Just thinking about those days made me cry. At school, my teacher knew something was wrong. I had no idea if she ever reported them, but I don't think she knew how hard it was for me at home. She was the most beautiful woman I had ever seen. Her skin was so dark and smooth with full features. She knew my stepmother was white and attributed my unkept hair to that. Once a week she would take my recess, wash my hair in the bathroom sink, blow dry, and braid it. Sometimes she had to help me wash under my arms and my privates because I came to school with an unpleasant odor. I could shower at home, but sometimes I would skip it because I hated bringing attention to myself. I stayed in my room and came out when it was time for school.

One day, my mom came to pick me up. She told my father she was back on her feet and wanted me home. There were some angry words exchanged, but I was too busy frantically throwing my stuff in a trash bag to hear what was said. My sister yelled for me as I ran out, but I didn't even look back or stop to hug her. I was filled with regret. I should've hugged and loved on Leanna; she was my only sibling, and I hadn't seen her since that day. There were never proper goodbyes or true closures for me. First my grandmother, then my mother, and now Leanna. That ten-year-old girl didn't realize the impact of the careless act of not saying goodbye and how it would haunt her.

My mother had a nice car and a beautiful three-bedroom home. I figured it was what she was doing when I was with my father. But a year later, her car broke down. She was making several calls to my father. I realized she didn't have the money to maintain everything. One day, my father came over and they started arguing. My mother sent me to my room and told me, no matter what, don't come out until she gets me. I knew the fight got physical, I heard a lot of stuff falling, bumping, and breaking. I put my headphones on.

Next thing I knew, my mom burst in the room, clothes torn, and face swollen. She snatched me up and hurried me to the neighbor's house. I saw the police and ambulance, but my neighbor closed the blinds and sent me to the back room. I wouldn't see my mother again for another two years. She went to jail for killing my father. Once again, no goodbyes.

It was no wonder I found it hard to form and break bonds. Every relationship I had was toxic or just broken with no warning. Growing up like that was why I hated being alone and hated to be attached to people at the same time. I was confused about what I should do with people and with myself.

"So, can you give me an example of you avoiding an emotional attachment now? You know you are in control of your relationships. You do not have anyone else pulling you here or there. You're the adult," Ms. Franklin said.

I couldn't answer that; it was so much. The first thing that came to mind was my casual relationships with men, mainly Mike and Roy.

"Not exactly. I just know I crave physically being with men. I like their attention; I like that they like me. But I'm attracted to men who could never be emotionally available to me. The risk is much lower when a man can't offer anything emotionally. As for friendships, I have few real friends, mostly associates."

"You are in a nonproductive cycle, aren't you? You want to form meaningful bonds, but bonding with people scares you, so you just deal with people who are unemotionally available. You can play this game with yourself forever. Do you understand what I am saying? We will definitely unpack that, but let's start with this. Forget about the men and how they like you. What about learning to like yourself so much that you realize you deserve someone available to you in every way. Everything you desire starts with you."

"Okay, I guess I just have to focus on fixing myself?"

"Don't look at it as fixing but working towards a future you want and deserve." She offered me her classic sad smile.

Sad was an appropriate description of my life. So, what did I do? Overeat, drink too much, smoke, and fuck away my emotions. Of course, it felt good for a moment then the next day, back to reality. Yea, I had bad habits, but I functioned okay. No one at work would ever guess I had issues, not even Daniel, my work husband. It's like my life was an embarrassing secret, full of meaningless sex and drama.

Having a life, I was too ashamed to share was tiresome. So, I gave in and worked toward a better me with no nightmares, no self-medicating, and no casual encounters. All the things I wanted I had control over. Ms. Franklin suggested tackling the nightmares and talking to my mother about my childhood. Having more than a superficial conversation with her wasn't going to be easy and I wasn't quite ready for that.

The easiest thing to do at this point was get rid of the *casuals* Mike and Roy, my guilty pleasures. I liked the attention and company they provided, and the power struggle I had with them was strangely satisfying. The after-effects of them wasn't good; they made me feel used and disposable sometimes. The risk of being hurt was inevitable.

I didn't feel safe with them, like I did with Johnathon. He and I spent several nights together. We leaned on each other emotionally. It was like crazy supporting crazy; if that wasn't dysfunction at its best, I didn't know what was. Johnathon acted totally straight to oblige his family. They were old school and didn't agree with being gay or bisexual. He endured camps and classes to make him straight and eventually left his hometown. Now, here he was, sadly happy. He was happily living as a single bisexual male, but sad without his family.

The nights Johnathon and I spent together could go either way—drinking, smoking, and laughing or lying there solemnly, holding each other, nursing our emotional wounds. Johnathon was the only man that showed gentleness to me in every way. He always treated me like fine china, and I loved him for that. We had slept together before, but those few times had been alcohol filled and a casualty of an unusually terrible day for one of us. He showed me what true love and friendship was supposed to feel like.

My plan was to let go of the *casuals* and work on becoming mentally, emotionally, physically, and financially healthy. I wanted to buy a house with a big patio so I could sit outside, and drink coffee or wine. The thought of not having Johnathon next door was unbearable and my anxiety consumed me when the idea came to mind. But I'd been stationary for way too long. It was time for me to grow up, settle my soul, and take my life back. Traveling the world would be nice, even if I did it alone. I looked forward to new beginnings and becoming the Leesha I was meant to be.

CHAPTER 5

Meeting the Michaels

I t had been four months since I let the *casuals* go. My life was pretty basic and boring, and I liked it that way. The only thing that entertained me was work. My boss still reminded me every day for three weeks to be ready for the Michaels, that prominent family. They were known for building multimillion dollar homes and their generosity to many charities. They may have been generous, but not very courteous in my opinion. How rude of them not to give a solid day, time, and make a real appointment.

The day finally arrived; I had opted for a cream pants outfit. The pants were slightly loose but still hugged my curves. The matching jacket had short sleeves with a little puff on the shoulders. I accented the outfit with a burgundy top and matching heels. My hair was pulled back into a sleek ponytail, and I wore dark red lipstick to emphasize my full lips.

I was sitting in my office with my shoes kicked off when the secretary came in and announced the arrival of the Michaels. I adjusted my attitude and walked out to meet them.

"Hello, it's nice to finally meet you all. I'm Leesha Roberts, the supervisor of Lotus Gardens." My smile was convincing as I shook the older lady's hand.

"Yes dear, aren't you a beautiful girl. Call me Francine," she said with a wide smile.

"Well, thank you very much. Is this your family?" I gestured to the younger woman and a man standing behind her wheelchair.

"Yes, this is my granddaughter, Katherine and her husband, Henry," she said with a little eye roll and a peculiar grin. "I wish to wait on my grandson, Karl. His plane got in late."

"Grandmother let's begin. Karl can catch up," Katherine suggested.

"Okay, if you insist." There was the eye roll again. "But no decisions are made without him. If you'll need to get rid of me, I want the appropriate people making decisions." She was a stern woman.

"Good grief, Grandmother! Get rid of you? Please! This was your idea. Anyway, I can assure you that no decisions will be made without Karl. Let's go."

I started my spill. "A little about Lotus Gardens, it's an assisted living facility on one side and an independent living facility on the other. The staff consists of registered and licensed nurses, nurse aids, housekeepers, and twenty-four-hour maintenance. We also have a full-service dining facility to include room service, a beauty salon, and daily exercise and activities."

Francine interrupted. "And you are a registered nurse?"

"Yes ma'am, with a master's in healthcare administration, so I wear several hats here."

"Oh, you must be very intelligent to be in charge of such a big facility."

"I like to think I can handle things okay."

"Are you from here?" Francine inquired.

"Actually, I moved here from Louisiana. I wanted a new start, so I came here after I graduated high school."

"Oh, so you've been on your own for a while! Smart, independent, beautiful, and a good aura. I like it." Francine grinned as she glanced at her granddaughter. Katherine remained unimpressed with the conversation.

I was done with the small talk. "Please follow me. We will tour the independent living side as requested." I gave the tour, showing the dining room, beauty shop, and activity room. Finally, we were going to her room when I heard a male's voice.

"Grandmother, I'm so sorry I'm late. Traffic was…"

"Stop with the excuses, Karl, you're always late. This is Ms. Roberts. It's Ms., isn't it?" She smiled as she gestured toward me, showing off her bracelets and shiny rings.

"Yes ma'am, it is." I shook Karl's hand.

"Nice to meet you." He greeted me.

He was a good-looking man with dark hair and emerald, green eyes, and a sexy ass five o'clock shadow filling his strong jawline. It looked like he had a nice physique under his tailored suit. He wasn't the type to be looking at a tall, thick Black woman, so I didn't know what his grandmother's smile was about.

"Well, let's look at what hopefully will be your apartment." My smile was genuine this time. I liked Mrs. Francine Michaels, she had character.

I led them into the large room with an area for a living and dining room set-up. There was a small kitchen with a stove, microwave, and polished cabinets. The bedroom was directly across from the kitchen.

"Well, what do you think?" I asked.

"It's okay," Francine said crudely. "I need Karl to have the full tour, but not now. I am tired and wish to go home. Karl will come back tomorrow, right before lunch, then you two can discuss it over a bite to eat. I insist and don't like back talk." Her words were final. She rolled away in her wheelchair.

Karl looked a little stunned then peered at me. His eyes traveled my body, stopping at my eyes. When our eyes met, I quickly diverted his gaze. "Okay then, I'll see you tomorrow around eleven o'clock, Ms. Roberts."

"Certainly, Mr. Michaels. I will gladly give you the complete tour tomorrow, but lunch is not necessary. I'm sure you're very busy." I was trying to back out of the uncomfortable situation. Francine's granddaughter sighed and walked away; her husband followed behind her.

"Grandmother doesn't like back talk," he said with a little smile, looking at me more closely. "I will see you tomorrow for the tour and lunch, Ms. Roberts."

"It's Leesha, but everyone calls me Lee, you can as well."

"You can call me Karl. Goodbye, Lee." His eyes spoke louder than his words, making my stomach tingle.

The rest of the day was uneventful. I told Daniel about the forced lunch date, which he quickly advised against. He reminded me that this was business, and I was asking for trouble if I go. He was always the voice of reason, but when did I ever listen to reason?

The next day, I kept my attire simple. I wore black dress pants, a semi-sheer ruffled shirt with a black tank top underneath, and black heels. Karl arrived on time. I was admittedly excited, but I didn't know why. I gave him the tour, but he wasn't really interested. After the tour was over, he asked if I had any idea where I wanted to eat. The lack of planning wasn't impressive but was obviously consistent with the Michael's style. I suggested somewhere quiet where we could discuss the possibility of his grandmother moving in. We settled on a small family-owned Italian restaurant close by. I didn't care that Karl was rich and we could've gone anywhere. I was hungry and didn't want to risk going to a high-class restaurant with one scallop and a teaspoon of spinach as a meal.

We sat in a small booth in the restaurant's corner.

"Thank you for agreeing to have lunch with me. My grandmother can be a little pushy, but no one ever pushes back. She's the queen, you will find out soon."

"Queen Francine, I can get into it." I laughed.

"Well, you better be ready, I think she likes you." He flashed a beautiful smile.

"I'm glad she likes me, she seems interesting, and I look forward to learning more about her."

"Careful what you ask for. I think I should let you know that Grandmother made her mind up about staying at Lotus Gardens a long time ago. That tour was just protocol for her. She couldn't care less about what I thought."

"That's strange. I'm sure she has everything she needs to stay in her own house. Do you know why she chose Lotus Gardens?"

"No, but I am sure she has her reasons. Anyway, tell me about yourself, Leesha."

"Well, besides being a supervisor at Lotus Gardens, I don't do much. I grew up in Louisiana and moved to San Antonio just for a change and to go to nursing school. I ended up finding a job and settling down here."

"Are you dating?"

"No, I am taking a break from the dating scene."

"Why do you need a break? I don't doubt you have a robust dating life, but so robust you need a break?"

"I wouldn't say robust, more like a meaningless dating life." I avoided Karl's eyes and studied my straw as I stirred my Coke.

"Isn't most dating meaningless in general?" I felt him looking at me.

"Yea, but I'm ready for more," I answered before I thought about what I said. "I mean, I wanna be alone and work on the self-love thing now." I looked up. Our eyes met and lingered on each other.

"Self-love thing? That's interesting. I can't imagine what you feel you should improve or fix about yourself. You seem pretty perfect to me." Karl's eyes searched my face.

"Well, we all could use a little self-improvement, but I just choose to actually focus on myself for a while. You know, shit like get healthy or whatever." I was trying to change the conversation.

"Of course." Karl took the hint.

"What about you, so are you dating? Or should I say do you have a robust dating life?"

Karl laughed. "I date a little when I have the time but stay busy with work for the most part."

"It's kinda hard to believe that you don't have a special someone or have multiple women pursuing you." I was curious about his dating life even though he looked like trouble for me. There is no way I could stay focused on myself with him around. The butterflies furiously fluttering in my stomach confirmed that I liked him.

"I have my share of women who claim to be interested in me, but like I said, no time. Or maybe I just haven't found the one I am willing to make time for."

"You made time for me." I joked but was hoping he was gonna catch what I was throwing.

"I did, I wanted to." Karl caught it. "Are you blushing?" My smile was like a schoolgirl talking to her crush.

"Oh God! I am blushing!" I grabbed my face and couldn't help but to laugh at myself.

Karl reached over the table and gently removed my hands from my face. "Don't cover your face, your smile is beautiful."

"Thank you." I regained my composure. "I'm sorry to be acting all giggly and stuff, but it's been a while since… well, since I've had such a nice time."

"I'm enjoying myself too, and yes, it has been a while for me as well." His smile was genuine.

"Anyway, I told you a little about myself, now tell me about you. How old are you? Do you have children? What do you do?" I hit him with the rapid-fire questions.

"Okay, I see you're getting right to the point. I'm thirty-four and have no kids yet. I'm too busy trying to prove that I can successfully run the family business, KM Construction. I travel and work with architects and design-ers to get different plans and materials. Our clients want unique touches if they are going to pay millions of dollars.

I have a good network established so things are getting redundant," Karl answered quickly.

"Redundant? Oh, so you need some excitement, right? I mean, at least at work." I tried not to fall into my old flirty self.

"I don't want excitement at work, but I could use excitement in my personal life."

"Oh, I'm sure a man like you can get all the excitement he wants."

"I can, but not always; I don't mind working for something I really want." His eyes sparkled.

I was officially nervous. My phone went off, and there was a message from Daniel asking if I was returning to work, it was already 2:45 p.m.

"I have to go. I didn't realize it was so late." I was slightly panicked.

"Aren't you the supervisor?" His eyes narrowed.

"Yes, but I'm not the boss or the owner, I can't just take the whole day for lunch," I said, grabbing my purse.

"Mark will understand, I'm sure. Tell him that Karl Michaels is holding you hostage if he asks."

"So, you know my boss, the owner's son?"

"We went to school together."

"Okay, I guess I'll stay. Let me text my co-worker back." I was hesitant but texted Daniel and let him know I wasn't returning today. He sent the eye roll emoji saying, "Seriously, Lee?" I ignored him and put my phone away.

Karl took that as a cue to order a bottle of wine. I let him know drinking wasn't on my agenda because I still had to drive home. He promised to get me home. Either he would drive, or he would get me a driver. I made a mental note to limit myself to two glasses so I could drive myself home; I wasn't sure he should know where I lived yet.

The conversation went on and time flew. He was so down to earth, nothing like I thought. He was fun, charming, and beautiful inside and out. We agreed that his grandmother was trying to hook us up.

"My grandmother does not like anyone I bring around, serious or not. She said the few women I introduced her to were superficial."

"Well, was she right?" I was curious.

"I didn't think so until she said that, then I became judgmental of everything they did." He laughed and shook his head. "It's rare she tries to set me up, but she is a good judge of character. She could tell almost anything about a person by looking at them."

"Can she tell I'm Black and you all hardly look like the kind of family that…" my voice trailed off. I didn't want to sound ridiculous.

"I said she is a good judge of character, not color blind. You're right about my family. There is not much variety, but my grandmother is cut from a different cloth. She doesn't follow the Michaels' rules. Honestly, her relationship with my grandfather's family was always a little strained. She is a free spirit, loves people, no matter where they are from, as long as they are good. Most people in my family don't see her that way." His eyes glimmered as he spoke about Francine.

I was happy that she saw me as a good person. If she only knew my truths, she would run Karl away from me as fast as she could. But I decided to just enjoy the remainder of the day and not take this lunch seriously. It was difficult because his charm was drawing me in. Butterflies continued their dance in my stomach when it was time to go. It was getting late, and I hated for the date to end. He stood up and grabbed my hand.

"I don't want this day to end," he confessed. "Since I don't have Grandmother to set me up, I guess I'll ask you out myself. Can we have dinner tomorrow night?"

"Sure, that would be nice. Let me know where and I can meet you." I remained cautious, making sure I didn't let him into my space too easily.

"Nonsense, I will send a car for you." He gave my hand a gentle squeeze. This man could make me break the rules. We settled on the dinner details. I opted for a church hug, but he held me close and made sure his lips brushed my neck. I exhaled nervously and he released his grip. "I apologize for being so touchy. See you tomorrow evening?" He looked a little nervous.

"You're fine, Karl, and yes, see you tomorrow evening." I played it off even though his hug caused my pussy to moisten. I had not felt that way in months. I went home, praying my rose was charged so I could release some of the pressure Karl built up.

The next day, I was in a great mood but also had a lot of anxiety. Daniel acted disgusted with me.

"You're getting your hot ass in a lot of trouble," he cautioned.

"Daniel! It's just dinner."

"Yea, dinner after a five plus hour lunch date! Lee don't start this. It's not rocket science; this is a terrible idea."

I ignored Daniel's warning and went on the date. I was stubborn and drove my own car. When I walked into Flemings Prime Steakhouse and Wine Bar a hostess met me at the door.

"Ms. Roberts?" she asked.

"Um, yes," I stuttered. *Why would she be waiting for me?*

"Right this way, ma'am." She ushered me to a private room in the back of the restaurant.

I became nervous, hoping the simple black wrap dress, jeweled stilettos, and clutch was nice enough for whatever was in store for me. My hair was straightened then curled giving a controlled curly look, with one side tucked behind my ear to add some sex appeal. I smoked my eyes with shimmery black and gray to highlight their honey color. My lip was painted with a simple gloss, and my good bra lifted the girls up.

Karl was waiting and stood up as soon as he saw me. "Leesha, you look beautiful. I'm glad you came." He pulled me in for a hug. This time, I melted right into his embrace. He wore black dress pants and a white collared shirt. His black jacket was hanging on the back of his chair. He smelled like vanilla, leather, and bergamot. I hadn't smelled that cologne before, but I could bury my face in his chest all night.

"Of course, I was coming. Thank you for inviting me." My cheeks were already getting sore from smiling so much.

He circled behind me and pulled my chair out. I felt his eyes travel down my body. My wrap dress was tied tight enough to accentuate my waist and emphasize my wide hips, ample ass, and shapely thighs. He walked back around the table and sat in his chair.

"You look amazing, Lee." His eyes glimmered. I noticed his five o'clock shadow was filling in nicely, and the sparkles in his eyes were accentuated by his dark hair.

"Thank you. You look very handsome. I didn't know we were going to have a room to ourselves." I glanced around and noticed we had our own private bartender. "Wow, this is so nice, Karl." No one had ever done something like this for me.

We ordered drinks and browsed the menu. Karl ordered sweet chili calamari as an appetizer. I settled on a Manhattan, and he ordered vodka and tonic. We selected the ribeye with the truffle -poached lobster on top. Our sides were the crispy bacon brussels sprouts and Flemings' potatoes. We laughed and talked about our jobs and bucket list plans as we enjoyed the delicious dinner.

"I really want to go to Turks and Caicos," I announced. I was a little tipsy by this time.

"Really? I will take you. Just say the word." Karl was serious when he said that.

I laughed. "Yea, right. I will be able to take myself one day, sir." I was still on the hands-off independence shit.

"Okay, if you say so." He laughed as he motioned for more drinks.

"Oh no, I'm done. I must cut myself off."

"You don't have to. The night is still young," he insisted.

I knew my limits. "I'll take water," I told the bartender. It was better to play it safe because I was known to get a little sloppy and didn't want to do that with Karl.

An hour later, we decided to call it a night. Karl grabbed my hand and kissed it instead of our newfound comfortable hug. "Lee, can I kiss you?" he asked.

Now the butterflies were swarming in my tummy. "Yes, Karl."

I was anxious to feel his lips on mine. My mind screamed a warning against this whole situation, but my gut said this was okay. I went with my gut. Karl kissed my forehead; his lips brushed my nose and then softly kissed my lips. Our mouths danced in a slow beautiful rhythm, tongues tasting each other. Karl's kiss was the most gentle and sensual kiss I'd ever experienced. I could tell he wanted to relish in the moment as much as I did. We reluctantly parted, both gasping. Karl's 6'4" athletic stature towered over me, but my head remained tilted up in effort to keep his gaze.

"I think you're trying to steal my heart, Karl Michaels," I confessed.

"I know you stole mine, Leesha Roberts," Karl said as he went in for another kiss. This one was more hunger filled. My center warmed as his hands slid to the small of my back. I shivered, thinking what it would be like to make love to him. His lips slid down and suckled my neck. I became lightheaded, drunk off of Karl's body, his soul.

Karl walked me to my car, and I was floating. I loved this feeling. He gave me one last kiss and opened my car door. I got in and he leaned down.

"I want to see you again." His smile was contagious.

"I would love to see you too. Call me so we can make plans." I returned his smile.

"Very well, I will call you soon."

I drove away on cloud nine.

I had no intention of letting Karl interfere with my journey. Resisting him would be a challenge, and he may not be around for long anyway. It was hard to believe that something this good could happen to me. I feared being his dirty little secret, especially if it was going to be a racial thing. There had been enough of that to last me a million years.

Naturally, Johnathon's opinion was needed.

"Damn Lee, you just dating the man; you aren't marrying him," Johnathon said.

"I know, but that's the point. I don't see any long-term thing happening and I'm not just throwing my pussy around, much less giving my time away for no reason."

"But how in the hell do you know if it will be long-term until you give the short-term a chance?"

Johnathon was right but that didn't stop me from being oppositional. "Look Johnathon, that rich white boy does not intend on keeping me around too long. You should see his sister's face when I'm there. That family definitely got some racism there, and I don't have the strength to deal with that."

"How you know what that white boy intends on doing? You ain't dating his sister anyway, so who gives a shit how she looks at you. Quit being ridiculous and give that man a chance, let him into that cold old heart of yours."

"Okay you don't have to get personal, Mr. Grinch that stole Christmas! Anyway, I will let him in…just a little bit."

I agreed to date Karl, just to see where it goes, but he wouldn't be my priority. I had a few more things to face, like my attraction to dysfunctional relationships and my father's death, which haunted me. After I deal with that, I would be free of everything that was holding me back from living a fulfilling life. Maybe when all this is over, I would run away, and go live in another country for a few months. Change was much needed, and a little adventure wouldn't hurt. Karl was a bonus prize.

CHAPTER 6

The Arrival of Fate

Karl and I had talked on the phone every night and texted several times a day. He texted me every morning, I checked on him mid-day, and we would end our days with flirtatious messages. I liked the distance we were keeping but was still becoming a little too attached to him. Unlike past relationships, he was taking his time getting to know me. I wasn't dependent on looks and sexual technique to keep him around, and that felt good.

It was the middle of April, and it was Fiesta Week in San Antonio. Lotus Gardens was decorated colorfully to prepare for the annual party. There was a variety of Mexican sweet bread readily available in several areas throughout the building. The residents were dressed in bright colors and excitement filled the hallways.

Of course, that was the day Francine started moving into the facility. Katherine and the movers arrived first. She wasn't shy about showing her irritation toward whomever crossed her path. Francine's furniture was the perfect size for her apartment. Her clothes were placed systematically in the closet and perfectly folded in the drawers. They properly hung family pictures on the wall along with some expensive looking art pieces. Katherine had overseen the whole move in. Of course, the real help was hired, so she did little but order people around. When I visited a couple of times to see how things were going, she gave me the cold shoulder.

Francine arrived when the move-in was complete. She appeared to be pleased with everything. Katherine was still there to make sure everything was to her liking. It was disappointing that Karl didn't show up. Francine announced everything was lovely, and Katherine could leave. I left right before she did.

The Fiesta festivities exhausted me, so I hid in my office for a while. Daniel was coming in later that day, so I had time to myself. I settled on the couch in the corner of my office. Soon there was a knock. I swung the door open just a little irritated. My heart thumped wildly when I saw Karl and was immediately nervous. He was wearing some rugged jeans, a white t-shirt, some work boots, and a cowboy hat. I was still a little tripped out that Karl was the total opposite of my type. He looked handsome, but the cowboy hat threw me off a bit.

"Good afternoon, Ms. Roberts." He smiled. "Did I catch you at a bad time?"

"No, Mr. Michaels. Please come in." Our formalities were on display for the secretary gawking at us.

Karl walked in, shutting the door, and locking it without hesitation. "Wow, aren't you ready to party." He eyed my long yellow skirt, white off the shoulder top with colorful embroidered flowers. My hair was in a puffy high ponytail with a white rose stuck in the side.

"Yes, the residents made Fiesta floats and we are having a parade later on," I explained.

Karl smiled. "You look gorgeous."

"Thank you, and you look fine in your cowboy hat and all."

Karl laughed. "That's right, you've never seen me dressed down. I had to visit some properties in the country to make sure things were going okay. But I wanted to see you. I've missed you." He eagerly kissed me. Our mouths did that familiar dance, taking us back to the last time we had seen each other. Again, his soft lips gently kissed my neck. I moaned, giving him reason to continue. His hands left my waist and traveled to my hips. I knew he was testing the waters to see how far he could go. I ran my fingers through his hair, encouraging him to keep going. His hands gripped my ass, and he gasped as his dick fought against the restraints of his jeans. My juices were flowing, saturating my black, lace panties. He backed me up against my desk, picking me up and placing me on top effortlessly. His strength turned me on, beyond reason. He rubbed and squeezed my thighs as kisses became more aggressive. He slowed down and whispered in my ear.

"Please, Leesha, I want you so bad. Let me make you feel good. Just tell me yes or no."

I wasn't that damn reformed, so of course I moaned, "Yes, whatever you want, baby." That shit drove him crazy. He lifted my flowy Mexican skirt with ease. I felt his fingers slide up and down the outside of my panties. They were wet as hell, turning him on more. He quickly pulled them to the side, gaining full access to play with my clit and completely explore my pussy. I kept her waxed, so I knew any experience with her would be more than pleasurable. Karl kneeled down and my body trembled. He licked the inside of each thigh as if he were doing a taste test then licked my middle. I gasped as Karl ate my pussy like it was his last meal. My body jerked and shivered, and my closed eyes only saw colorful swirls of light as Karl's mouth took me to the edge. I put my hand over my mouth to muffle my scream as I came.

"You are delicious, Leesha." His hooded eyes looked like he was the one about to pass out.

"Are you done?" I panted.

"I don't want to be," he responded.

I reached down, feeling the enormous bulge in his pants. "Then don't be." He understood what I meant. Karl undid his pants, releasing his manhood. He was well endowed with a long, thick dick. I was about to go fucking crazy. He pulled a condom from his wallet and slid it on. I whimpered as he entered me. Our connection was emotional. Even though we were being nasty, fucking on my desk, I felt intertwined with something beyond the physical. I was in bliss. Karl slowly stroked my pussy until he couldn't hold back anymore. His pace increased, and I met his rhythm as our bodies danced until we both exploded. I could tell Karl had been waiting for that release, and quite frankly, so had I. He withdrew, letting his manhood fall. We just stared at each other thinking, *what just happened?*

"Sorry," he apologized. "I really didn't want our first time to be in your office, I wanted to romance you." His laugh was nervous.

"It's okay. You felt so good, Karl, I missed you too. But you got to go, Daniel will be here any minute." We opened the door and thankfully the secretary was nowhere in sight. I pointed the way to our office restroom and Karl hurried in. I opened the door wide to the office, sprayed some of my Jimmy Choo perfume and turned on the fan to blow the smell of sex out of there. Karl reappeared looking just as good as he did when he first arrived.

"I'm going to go see Grandmother for a second," he said.

I rushed over to kiss him goodbye, trying to hurry him away. When he left, I ran to the restroom to clean myself up, wash my panties, and dried them with the hand dryer. *Leesha you at work fuckin'! Shame on you*, I silently scolded myself.

Daniel arrived to work about an hour later. "Smells good in here. What perfume is that?" he asked.

"It's Jimmy Choo. I have been running all day with this Fiesta business and had to freshen up," I overexplained.

"Yea, I see all that sweet bread everywhere. Blood sugars are going to be through the roof. I would tell the nurses to make sure all Accuchecks are done. Even check in with the residence in independent living to make sure they check theirs. It's going to be insulin city tonight." He laughed.

"Ain't that the truth!" I agreed.

Later that day, I was sitting at my desk and Daniel was showing me pictures of his home that was being remodeled. We had the good coffee from the café down the street. I loved moments like this, it was so relaxing. My desk phone rang, breaking the vibe we had going. I answered in a sophisticated voice.

"Leesha Roberts please." It was Francine.

"Yes ma'am, this is Leesha. What can I do for you?"

"Can you come to my place, please?" She was pleasant but demanding.

"Sure, is everything okay?"

"Everything is fine, dear. I want to talk to you."

I told Daniel that Francine wanted to see me. We both had the "oh, hell" look on our faces.

Daniel mocked. "See, you had a meal with her grandson and now she thinks she can call you anytime. Not appropriate."

I've had more than a meal with Karl, but he was right. I hoped this didn't become a habit. There was a button she could push if she needed help. One of the attendants or nurses would respond to her immediately. She was easily the richest resident we had but having me on call wasn't the answer. She could've stayed in her home if she wanted service like this.

I knocked, and she opened the door. It surprised me to see she was standing and not in the wheelchair. She welcomed me in and offered me a seat. The smell of burned sage floated around the room.

"Excuse the smell, dear. I had to get rid of the unwanted spirits, the bitches, witches, and such." There was that smile again. She went to the kitchen and came out holding a silver tray with a pink and silver tea set up. The set wasn't the standard plain flowered kind. It was swirled with different shades of pink and shiny silver. It was unique and beautiful. But the beauty of that set didn't distract me from the fact that she intended for me to stay for a while.

"Have a seat and enjoy some tea with me," she suggested.

I sat down, wondering how to get out of this. But that smile she had given me earlier kind of made me want to stay. She was an interesting character and I wanted to know more about her. She sat the tray down, glided to her wheelchair, lifted the cushion, and took out a small bottle of Canadian Mist. *Not the most expensive shit, but it will fuck you up*, I thought to myself.

She sat down and did a little shake of the bottle. "Would you like some, my dear?"

"No ma'am, just tea is fine. How are you liking the place so far?"

"It's okay. I can be happy anywhere though. I have my reasons for coming here."

That made me curious. "What are your reasons? I'm sure you had a lovely home."

"I have a lovely house, not a home."

This sounded like something I didn't have time to get into. So, I didn't pursue it. I watched her pour a little bit of the Mist in her teacup then she poured tea in both cups. She smiled, picked up the cup, with a small cheer in my direction, and took a sip.

"Tea is served. Have a taste. It's raspberry with a hint of lavender infused honey. Have you heard from Karl lately? He said he enjoys your company. I can tell, you make him happy. Why don't you two go out more? I know you are going to be great together. I just don't know what you are waiting for. Life is so very short, my dear. He is a good man. Take him! Don't leave him sitting for the next simple bitch to snatch his ass up!" The urgency in her voice didn't offer me any time to answer her questions.

"Where is all this coming from? Surely, I'm not the type of woman your family would want to be with Karl for any real amount of time. He's nice and handsome but I'm working on myself and dating a man whose sister already dislikes me is not a good introduction back into the dating scene. I like Karl, but that scares me."

My mouth was saying all the right things, but deep down I wondered where it would go if I did pursue Karl. I wasn't ready to seriously date this man right now. I could've fixed my shit a long time ago, but at this point all I thought I would do was sabotage the whole thing. We really liked each other, but never said we were serious or exclusive. But now we recklessly added sex to the equation. Not just sex, this was the type that made me nervous. Our connection was emotional now.

"You know what?" Francine sat next to me. "Without our experiences, our flaws, our fuckups, we wouldn't have a story. So what? A man's family is not expecting a woman like you. The Michaels were not expecting a woman like me either. Believe me, I wasn't what my husband's family wanted. I was poor and raised by my older sister. She worked odd jobs to care for me. She even sold her body sometimes, just to make sure I ate. She was considered the lowest of the low in our community. She was a lot of men's secret fantasy, but I looked up to her. She was generous, caring, and hard-working. Her reputation followed me, and the Michaels hated me. By that time, my sister was married to a dependable laidback man, and I was working at the local bar. They assumed I sold my body too. I didn't care because I never saw the shame in it anyway. It paid for our food. We needed to eat, but those men didn't need sex to live. Somehow our needs were worse than their wants. Now you have a little of my story. I have lived an interesting life." Francine was becoming an open book, but I was still closed. She had no clue Karl and I had reached another level.

She stood up, walked to an unpacked box, and pulled out a bottle of wine, a brand I didn't recognize. She announced,

"This bottle is 15 years old. I'm opening it with you, this evening, cause you're worth it. You must learn that. It's a fact, you are worthy of everything you want!"

She glided to the freezer and put the bottle in. I want you to come this evening, so I can read your cards." She reached in her purse and pulled out an old, ragged deck of cards and gave me a wink.

How could I turn that offer down? I was excited. What was attracting Francine to me? Why her beloved grandson? Why a Black woman? Questions were running through my mind. I agreed to come back and planned to bring dinner.

That afternoon I got home, showered, and fussed a little about what I should wear. I settled on black leggings and a flowy peach colored blouse with gold hoop earrings to accent. We planned for dinner at 7:30 p.m. I had no idea what kind of food Francine liked. People her age were picky eaters. I didn't want to bring something she would absolutely hate. I decided to call Karl to ask what Francine liked. The phone rang three times before he answered, sounding happy.

"Leesha, hey baby, how are you?"

"I'm fine, just calling you to see what your grandmother likes to eat. I'm taking her dinner this evening."

"Okay, what a great welcoming committee you are. Do all your new residents get this attention or does she have something up her sleeve? Be careful with her, she is not the innocent old lady people think she is."

"Well … she offered to read my cards, and I thought it would be nice to bring her dinner." I was hesitant to say what our plans were, but Francine didn't seem like the type to care.

"Are you sure you're ready for a reading? She has never been wrong, hints the good judge of character. She has a way of taking you to places you never wanted to go to in the past and surprising the hell out of you about your future. It's quite unsettling. Many people say they can't sleep for days thinking about her readings."

"Now I'm just curious," I confessed.

"Grandmother is not a big eater. She's more of a grazer. That Italian spot we went to was good. Get her that grilled Tuscan steak and those antipasto skewers we had. I know she has the wine. Good luck with your reading. What are you doing later tonight after you leave her place? It's already established that you won't be sleeping. I can come by and get your mind off things."

It took me by surprise, but it was no use in playing hard to get now. Francine was right, life was too short. "Oh…okay," I stuttered. "Do you want to come by, or meet somewhere?"

I looked around my little apartment and realized I may have made a mistake asking him about coming over.

"It'll be late, we can do your place. Should I bring something?"

"No, I'll be full and probably a little tipsy later on." I laughed nervously.

We said our goodbyes and I headed to the restaurant to grab the food.

CHAPTER 7

Cutting Cards of the Past

I quickly walked to Francine's door after parking in the back of the building. I didn't want any of the employees or residents to see me there. I was hearing Daniel's "not appropriate" in my head, but my heart was telling me I needed this.

When Francine opened the door, she was striking. I immediately felt underdressed. Her hair hung loose like silver waves floating down her back. Her lips were painted red, and her green eyes sparkled against the candles placed around the room. She wore a long, black, flowing dress with silver embroidered flowers decorating the neckline.

"Come in, dear. I'm so glad you came. You are my first real guest! I love entertaining, especially when I don't have my grandchildren or the hired help looking over my shoulder." She took the bag and floated into the kitchen. "Let me set the food up, you can open the wine, my arthritis is acting up."

The apartment smelled of jasmine with a hint of vanilla. Accompanying the candlelight was a lamp in the corner with a sheer red scarf draped over the top. I pulled the wine out of the ice bucket she had sitting on the table. I was careful opening the bottle because I didn't want to spill a drop of the fifteen-year-old wine. I poured some in the glasses sitting next to the bucket. Francine sat the plates of steak in front of the only two chairs at the table. She left and reappeared carrying a glass serving tray with the antipasto skewers and the seasoned flat bread I added to the order. I could tell she loved entertaining. She complimented me on the dinner selection, and I confessed to calling Karl for guidance. She was obviously happy about that, but I decided not to disclose the plans we had for later that night.

We filled dinner with great conversation about Francine's travels she had with her late husband. When we finished eating, she pulled her cards out. There was a glimmer in her eye as she asked, "Ready, dear?"

"I guess so." I took a deep breath.

She spread the cards out and stirred them all over the table then gathered them up, making a neat deck. She shuffled them again, this time in a neat, organized manner, then placed them on the table.

"Cut them three times." Her voice was soft.

I carefully divided the stack placing one next to the other. My heart beat harder as I rubbed my sweaty hands together.

Francine pointed to the first deck, second deck, then the third deck. I leaned in as she began to speak.

"This is your past, present, and future." She stopped for a second and looked at me. It felt like her eyes were penetrating my soul. She flipped the top card over in each deck and laid them right above the stacks. She paused and gently touched each card as if they were speaking to her. Then she spoke.

"You had problems with past relationships. You were leaving a piece of yourself with that one, this one, and that one. You are now looking to become whole within yourself and then be whole for your life partner."

I gave no reaction because I didn't want her to play off of my emotions.

She flipped the top card of the past over. "A lot of sexual energy is involved in these lost relationships, but it's okay. Talk to your mother, she will be the biggest help. You will soon be over the sadness of your past." She flipped another card. "Your heart has been wounded, and you may be dealing with inadequacies."

So far everything she said was true, but nothing I wanted her to pick up on. This was getting a bit uncomfortable. The reading continued to the point where I couldn't tell which pattern the cards were being pulled, but she was spot on with everything. She advised me not to be hard on myself, to go to sleep earlier, travel, live free, don't be afraid, and don't be so emotional because it scared people.

I felt weird when she told me several men desired me and I crave the attention; it would take the right one to take away that craving. She said my future is here, don't push it away, be accepting and not afraid. My past would bless me in the future; it would be overwhelming, there would be much pain, but I would be okay. She also said I was going to have a lot of money someday. It would be all mine and there would be people cursing me.

"You will suffer losses, terrible ones. But you will find the strength to move on. One of those losses you will endure alone." Francine looked concerned.

There were other things said, but my mind dwelled on just those parts. When I was getting ready to leave, she gave me a tight hug and told me to pray. She also informed me that the reading wasn't too specific, but the choices I make would dictate my paths.

CHAPTER 8

Complicated Acceptance

When I got back home, I changed into a spaghetti strapped lounging dress and took a few minutes to pull a flat iron through my hair, enhancing the shine and displaying the length. I added a light blush, nude lip gloss, eyeliner, and mascara. Francine's reading got to me because here I was, taking extra care of my appearance tonight. Well, to be really honest with myself, it was probably Karl's dick that got to me. I lit some candles, straightened up the couch pillows, wiped down the coffee table, and put a bottle of Stella Rosa in the freezer. Nerves were already setting in when he texted letting me know he was on his way.

After Karl's text I got one from Roy: *Hey Lee, what's up with you? I miss you. Please hit me back, stop ignoring me.* I had no reason to answer, Roy was old news now.

When I heard the light knock on the door, butterflies fluttered in my stomach. I opened the door and there stood Karl, in all his stunning glory. He was holding some beautiful bright pink and yellow roses, and a cute bag with a bottle of wine in it.

"I saw these and thought of you, bright and beautiful. I hate coming to someone's home empty handed. I know you probably had enough to drink with Grandmother, but here's some wine anyway." He eyed me up and down as he spoke.

"Thank you so much. Come in." I took the flowers and wine and opened the door wider, allowing him to walk through. He smelled so good. Karl was wearing some dark denim jeans, and a white T-shirt, covered with an open black button-down.

"Your place is nice." He studied my small two-bedroom apartment.

My apartment was simple. It was decorated with a black leather couch and loveseat with a glass table set held up by curvy wrought iron. My coffee table had a silver tray of candles as a centerpiece. The candles matched the cream throw rug with black, beige, and rose-colored flowers. My walls had pictures with motivational quotes and scriptures. The kitchen had dark marble countertops, a tiny island, and stainless-steel appliances.

"Thank you." I placed the flowers in my only crystal vase and set them in the middle of the kitchen island. I complimented the beauty of the flowers again. Honestly, I couldn't remember the last time someone gave me some.

His bottle of wine was already chilled, so I poured us a glass. I needed something to settle my nerves.

"What kind of music do you like?" I broke the awkward silence.

"Mostly country," he said.

"You can link your phone to my system and play some country if you want, I don't mind," I insisted.

"No, just play whatever you have been listening to lately," Karl said.

I put on my mix of R&B, the perfect background music, plus I could sing along to my favorites. I sat down on the love seat across from the couch, took a sip of wine, and gave him what I thought was a seductive smile. Hopefully, he couldn't tell I was super nervous; texting was so much easier. Now there was an awkwardness between us, undoubtedly caused by our sexual encounter in my office.

"You're beautiful, Lee," Karl said, returning my smile.

"Thank you."

"I'm not playing or trying to be corny. I think you're beautiful inside and out. I get really excited when I know I'm going to see you."

"I feel the same way." I took another sip of wine.

This time his eyes peered at me as if he were expecting me to say something more. One thing he would soon learn about me was I wasn't a conversationalist, not good with words, or expressing my feelings.

"So, tell me about your reading. I mean whatever you are comfortable with telling me."

"Where do I start? Francine said so much. But every-thing was totally true and it's weird to know there is some-one on this earth with so much insight about me. There is some shit to deal with before I can move on and be happy. I'm also scared of what might happen."

I was focusing on my glass as I spoke, unwilling to make eye contact, afraid that he would want to leave because I was making the conversation heavy. So, I decided to lighten things up.

"But anyways, I'll tell you the good things that were in my reading."

"No, tell me what you started, what scares you, that is if you are comfortable. I'm a good listener. Maybe if you get it off your chest, you actually will sleep tonight." He picked up the remote and turned the stereo down.

I told him everything except the men and sexual energy parts. It wasn't like I was some innocent virgin, but he didn't have to know all the dirt. I did tell him what Francine said about my past and my mysterious upcoming losses.

I thought when I looked up at him, his eyes would show pity, but no, his eyes were understanding and seemed to be searching me. He was searching my soul, wanting to figure me out, like he just wanted to know me. This man spoke with his eyes more than anything.

"What are you thinking? I know, this is too much, right?" Nervous energy was kicking in again. "Anyway, do you dance?" By now the music was a mixture of everything, even my white girl stuff. *Every Rose has its Thorn* by Poison was starting. My mother always played this song. It made her sad, but it didn't stop her from having it on repeat from what I remember.

"Yea, I dance." He stood up and offered his hand to me.

I got up and placed one arm around his neck and my other hand slid into his. I avoided eye contact of course, but he was staring straight at me…waiting. Finally, I looked at him, that gaze couldn't be avoided. My body then melted into his and we slowly swayed. I loved this song, a tribute to our imperfections, alone and in relationships. Karl slowly rubbed my back, not in a seductive way, but in a way to comfort me, as if he could feel my sadness. My eyes were closed by this time, and I wanted to stay there forever. The song ended but we remained as if it were still playing.

"Leesha, you know…" He seemed to be searching for what he wanted to say.

"I know what?"

"You know that you're safe with me. I like you, and I won't hurt you."

Francine was right. Her grandson was intense, and I didn't know how to take this. I wanted to act unaffected by this whole scene and was afraid of what was becoming of us. I didn't want to go down this road, not with him or anyone. But this road was unfamiliar, carefully built, wanting me to take the chance and just walk on it.

My soul summoned my mouth to finally speak. "I know I'm safe." My mind was imploring me to say I wasn't interested in this mess. I wasn't equipped for this right now and needed to focus on me. Then I heard Francine say, "The one that truly loves you, will help you face your fears." Maybe Karl was the one for this season of my life, the one to break down that fear I had of relationships.

The night progressed and I was uneasy about what was said, but at peace with the fact that this felt right. Karl told me why his grandmother wasn't a fan of many people in his family and why everyone still tried to please her. To the family's dissatisfaction, Karl's grandfather had left the family's fortune to Francine, rightfully so; she was his wife. But according to Karl, people didn't think she was a good wife and deserved very little. He spoke of his childhood and memories of the younger Francine and how she rubbed everyone the wrong way.

Other than family drama, his life was full of traveling and doing what rich country boys do. Karl was the 'going to the rodeo and hunting trips' type of country. Definitely not my type. But the way he touched my hand, looked into my eyes, squeezed me tight when we hugged, and the way he dicked me down in my office was steadily making me weak.

It was late and I was exhausted. Karl was tired too and decided to call it a night. He walked to the door, and I followed. He turned and looked into my eyes with that "ask me to stay" look. I grabbed his hands and softly said my goodbyes. He leaned in and gave me the gentlest kiss ever. By this time, the wine had me relaxed enough to effortlessly kiss him back. When it was over, he leaned his forehead into mine and took a deep breath. The aroma of sweet wine settled into my nose. I wondered if my gasp was as delightful as his. Apparently, it was, because he leaned in for another kiss. This one was passionate, this one I craved.

I pulled away. "I had a nice evening."

"I did too. When can I see you again?" He was direct.

"I don't know." I was ambiguous. Of course, my phone vibrated again with a text. It had vibrated about three times during his visit. He glanced toward the phone, then at me.

"Okay, you can call me then." Karl stepped back with an intense expression that could've easily been mistaken for being a little pissed. Karl wasn't into playing hard to get, his life was way too busy for that. Even though I hadn't planned on doing the dating or sex thing now, I felt the need to adjust my tactic. I wasn't seeking his approval, but I was trying not to ruin our vibe.

"I can cook dinner for you, tomorrow night if you're free." I was doing the most now. I'd had a tough week and really wanted to chill all day tomorrow. I went from nonchalant to eager. Why was I afraid of him not liking me? Was it that fear of abandonment and rejection shit? I decided not to over analyze this situation. "How does 7:30 sound?"

"Well, I did have another engagement, but I just canceled that."

"I can do it another day, it's fine. I'm sure my little meal won't be as good as whatever you had planned." I was disappointed but kind of relieved.

"Why would you say that? My plans were good, but I'm choosing you, that's it. See you tomorrow evening." He opened the door, gave me a quick glance, and walked out.

Karl was a challenge and a distraction to my plans. I did want to see him more often but didn't want to fall into the pattern of uncommitted sex. At this point, I had to just trust myself with my decisions about him, and ignore distractions, like Roy. So, I mentally opened the door to allowing Karl into my world.

CHAPTER 9

The Unbreakable is Broken

The next morning, I woke up inspired. I called this feeling "Johnathon inspired." I put my music on and started cleaning. I vacuumed, swept, dusted, and polished my furniture. My place looked and smelled fabulous. I turned the music down and wondered why Johnathon had not called or texted me, impressed with my early morning energy. Come to think of it, I hadn't talked to him in a few days, which was a rarity in our relationship. I decided to go to his place and hoped he didn't have company.

When he opened the door, he was in pajama pants and a T-shirt. He looked tired and it was dark inside. Something was off. Maybe he had a long night; maybe he was sad or had a broken heart. He wasn't serious about anyone that I knew of.

"Hey friend, long time no see," I said, looking him up and down. "What is wrong with you? You look a steaming hot mess."

He rolled his eyes and opened the door to let me in. "Well, thank you, Ms. Early Morning, finally got your ass up to clean your house, sunshine."

When I walked in, the air felt sad and heavy. I flopped down on the couch. "No, for real, what's wrong, Johnathon?" I caught a glance at some boxes in the corner and sat up. "What are those boxes for?" I felt anxious; my heart had traveled to my throat, making it hard to breathe.

"Just packing up some old stuff." He sat down next to me and put his arm around my shoulders. He was never outright touchy feely for no reason. Fear started to set in as I laid my head on his shoulder. He swallowed hard as he squeezed me tighter. For reasons unknown to me, tears clouded my eyes.

"Johnathon, you are scaring me, what's wrong?" He said nothing. "Friend! What's wrong?" Panic was setting in. Once again, I was having a strong reaction and didn't know why.

"Leesha, please, don't do the drama queen shit. It's too early." His words were his normal, but his tone wasn't.

"Okay, but I know you, Johnathon. I feel you; I feel when your spirit is disturbed. Don't bullshit me. What the fuck are those boxes, why are you just waking up?" I couldn't breathe and now in a full-blown anxiety attack. "Why are you lying? Are you leaving me?" My heart pounded and head started to ache.

He stood up and held my face in his hands, forcing me to look at him. He started taking deep, slow breaths. That was his way of calming me. I put my hand on his chest and mirrored his breathing, closed my eyes, and whispered, "I'm okay, I'm okay."

"You will always be okay, you hear me. Leesha, you are my best friend. The best thing that has ever happened to me. Don't get all panicky on me; you're okay."

I started shaking my head, but my mouth couldn't say no.

"Lee, I'm moving back home. My mom is getting older, and I need to spend time with her."

"When? I'll go with you. Please wait for me. I've got to get my shit together and take off with you. I really have nothing holding me here." My drama continued.

"Silly girl, you have a good life, a good job, and you're doing great. What the hell are you going to do in fucking Arkansas? We still have time. I'm leaving next month. No crying, just fun for us. You can visit me there later."

What in the hell was going on? That was the worst break-up ever. I thought our bond, our friendship, could never be broken. In my mind, we were going to live out our lives as forever friends. I needed Johnathon. We had been through too much. We helped each other survive broken childhoods, broken hearts, and new jobs. We were two broken people and being together made us whole, and complete.

"Okay." I agreed with his plan. But in my mind, I had a plan to do whatever it would take to make him stay. I was going to change his mind. Yes, selfish me was trying to make him choose me over his own mother.

I spent the next few hours lying in Johnathon's bed talking. Turns out, his work crush was married with children but was open to messing around with Johnathon.

"I'm not a damn homewrecker!" The whole idea insulted him. "Much less being a secret lover to a so-called straight man. Give me a break." His tone was sad. Maybe that was why he was ready to leave. His love life was challenging, harder than mine because he dealt with women and men.

When he inquired about my life, I updated him on Karl and Francine. I wanted to take him to see her before he moved. He was into that card reading stuff, but he said he didn't need his cards read, and just wanted to live in the present, just hanging with me was good enough. That was just what I wanted to hear. Deep down my nervous system was going crazy. How could I keep on the right path without Johnathon to lean on? Only time would tell if I continued to be my own worst enemy.

CHAPTER 10

Unnecessary Insecurity

didn't feel like cooking or having company, but I promised Johnathon I would keep my date with Karl. He promised to make peach cobbler for my dinner. I made chicken stuffed with spinach, mushroom, and cream cheese with roasted potatoes on the side. I prepared a salad with vinaigrette dressing, put some beer in the freezer, and chilled some wine.

I asked Johnathon to join us, but of course he declined. I was okay with that because in my delusional mind he wasn't moving anyway. There was no way he could leave me. He was just going through some kind of crisis. A visit with his mother was all he needed, and he would be back home, back to our normal.

He helped me pick out my outfit and insisted on red lipstick. I thought that was a little much, but he said it was just enough. It was 6:15 and I started getting ready. I over applied my Gucci Guilty perfume, and under applied my make-up. I decided to let my hair dry naturally, added some product to tame it, and tossed it to the side. I put on black capris and a v-cut shimmery black shirt. Johnathon sat in the oversized chair in the corner of my bedroom. He gave me a smile of approval, got up to grab my glittery lotion, and despite my protest; he applied it to my cleavage. After he applied the lotion, he ran his fingers through my hair, lifted my chin, and gave me a lingering kiss. This was kind of weird to me.

"You look beautiful." His lips were still close to mine, then he gave me another kiss.

"You're perfect and I hope you know that."

I didn't say anything. I just looked at him. I wanted to tell him I was going to cancel with Karl, and he should stay with me, but I knew he wasn't for my intense neediness tonight. We were too good of friends and wanted each other to be happy. For us, it was a safe intimacy. He was always my security blanket, but sex made things weird with us. I backed away and half smiled at him.

"You're messing up my lipstick." I tried to laugh it off, but my eyes started to sting from the threat of tears.

"Well, let me get out of here so you can be ready for your date." His voice was filled with fake excitement.

"I'll call you when he leaves," I assured him.

"Don't bother. I'm going out with my co-workers tonight."

"What? You didn't tell me you were going out." I was glad he had plans.

"You didn't know because you weren't invited."

"Oh, okay. There's the bitch I know and love."

"Goodnight." He gladly let himself out.

I turned toward the mirror and realized I did look pretty. I had just enough shimmer to draw in Karl's eyes. My lips were the perfect contrast to my all-black outfit. I added some silver earrings, a thin silver chain, then slipped on my black jeweled flip flops.

When Karl arrived, his dark jeans and dress shirt made me feel underdressed. But his look of approval put me at ease. He brought me a beautiful bouquet of red roses in an elegant crystal vase. He smelled wonderful and I was kind of glad I overdid the Gucci perfume.

"Have a seat." I nodded toward the table. "I made stuffed chicken. Do you prefer wine or beer?"

"I'll do beer. Stuffed chicken, fancy, I'm curious to see if you can cook."

"Well, I cook damn good. I don't have all this body for nothing," I joked, trying to hide my insecurity.

"I love your body. I love everything about you." His eyes sparkled as he stared at me and opened his beer.

I felt my face grow hot as I prepared our plates.

"You're blushing. It's cute."

"Cute is not what I was going for." I turned toward him and was startled. He was right in my face. God! This man was too intense. His eyes pierced mine.

"What were you going for?" he asked.

Before I could answer, his lips hungrily pressed against mine. He started to run his fingers through my hair and quickly realized my hair wasn't the type you just run your fingers through. It had dried and looked nice but didn't submit to his hands. His attempt to loosen my coils turned into a purposeful, gentle pull. His kiss grew more commanding as he backed me up into my marbled counter then he loosened his grip and backed off.

"Sorry, I couldn't help it, I've been holding back since last night," he confessed.

"It's okay." I grabbed a napkin and slowly wiped his lips. He was trying to make me break all my rules. "Umm. Let's eat, tell me what you think," I suggested.

"I'm sure everything will taste great." He took a sip of beer.

Karl was indeed impressed with my cooking. I knew my way around the kitchen. I did give Johnathon the credit for the peach cobbler.

"You know, a woman has never cooked for me before. Usually, they want to go out to eat. I don't mind taking a woman out, but I could get used to this. Everything was delicious," Karl complimented.

"Thank you, I love to cook, but don't get to showcase my skills that often."

"Well, you can showcase your skills for me anytime."

"So, tell me more about the women you usually date? What's your type? Have you ever dated a Black woman?"

"No, but does it matter?"

"I'm curious. There are cultural differences, and we just maintain ourselves differently."

"Honestly, I don't know how women maintain themselves anyway, white, or black. As long as they look nice and smell good." Karl laughed.

"Ok, but why now and why me? Be honest."

"How do I explain what draws me to you? Besides you're down to earth, I feel like I can talk to you about anything, you're sexy as fuck, and…. I don't know, you just make me happy, Lee." Karl was looking down, but when he looked up our eyes locked and a warm sensation flooded my body. Then he smiled, causing me to melt. "Besides, Grandmother is crazy insistent that I pursue you. She really likes you for whatever reason. Like I said before, she thinks I should break from my norm, to find the one."

"Okay, I guess I'll be the first to break your norm," I teased, not dare wanting to mention being the 'one.'

"Speaking about norms, what about you dating white guys? Am I the first one you went out with?"

"I mean.. I've flirted with white guys or whatever, but never dated one. I already told you my father was white, and he wasn't very nice to me. It's kind of hard for me to see white guys as genuinely interested in me. I don't think all white men will mistreat me, but my father instilled in me that I wasn't good enough for any man, especially a white one. It's like he saw me as my mother when he said those things. I was a child and didn't know or care about men wanting me; I just wanted him to love me like he did my sister. It was just a crazy situation that made me avoid certain types of men as I got older, that included white ones. I just don't want to deal with that unnecessary insecurity," I admitted.

"So, your father was strict and basically lied to you about men in general, just to make you feel shitty and insecure?"

"Strict? No, he was straight up mean, that meanness…. no, that hatred was reserved for me, because my mother is Black. I was a mistake in his eyes. Needless to say, that's why I consider myself Black, not mixed or anything like that." I felt like breaking down and Karl grabbed my shaking hands.

"Lee, you don't have to say anymore. But I will tell you that your father is not a comparison to me. You are easily the best thing that has happened to me in a very long time, and I hate seeing you get so upset."

"I'm sorry. Talking about him just works me up. Sad thing is, I can't even talk to him and get an explanation, an apology…nothing. My mom made sure of that. So, now all I can do is sit in these crazy emotions when I think about him. I even have nightmares of him screaming at me. I'm sorry, you didn't ask all this." My eyes were fixed on our hands.

"I never want you to feel like you can't talk to me, say anything you want. You have a lot to get off your chest and I'm here. So how did your mother get tied up with your father?" Karl asked.

"She was working at a grocery store, and he always came in, trying to talk to her. She finally gave in and basically became his dirty little secret, but he didn't bet on her getting pregnant. He wined and dined her, made empty promises and here I am, a casualty of their fling."

"Well, I'm grateful for their fling and I'm grateful you were strong enough to get through all that craziness. Now you're here with me and I intend on taking good care of you and your heart." Karl softly held my face and gave me a gentle kiss.

I felt relieved after I got that out. The remainder of the night was nice. He became comfortable and seemed right at home. It was weird because it was rare I had a man sitting around my place just chilling with no obvious intention of jumping my bones. Usually, they were sitting there fighting a hard dick, invading my space, and hoping to get fucked, or maybe even knowing they would get fucked. I guess I set myself up like that. No attachments.

Our conversation went from serious to light-hearted. Karl was winning me over, but not enough to break my promise to myself. I was detoxing from everything that wasn't beneficial in my life and besides the office slip up, I was happy with my progress. But it was obvious Karl was trying to be around for a while.

He asked me to go to a black-tie charity event in two weeks. Shit, I have only seen events like that on TV. I happily agreed to go. My thoughts became fixated on what I would wear and how much weight I should attempt to lose.

The night ended with a long kiss that attempted to journey to my neck. But I stopped it, and we said our good-nights. After he left, my mind began to wander. *Does he just want to shock his crowd with the curvy Black chick? Does he just want to experience a sexual relationship with me just for kicks? What is it?* And there it was, that unnecessary insecurity.

CHAPTER 11

Regaining Stability

Johnathon was leaving me, and Karl had me weak and confused. I had to get my footing back, so I visited Ms. Franklin and updated her on my boring but crazy life. I spoke of the irrational overwhelming feelings of panic and anxiety when Johnathon told me he was moving back home. Honestly, the fear of losing him made me feel crazy, abandoned, and angry. I was angry he never mentioned he was thinking of moving back home. To me that was betrayal. That wasn't how we were with each other; he had broken that unspoken promise we made to each other.

"So, how did you feel when Johnathon told you he was leaving?" Ms. Franklin asked.

"Very afraid, anxious. It was like I couldn't breathe. He is such a big part of my life. Who will I talk to, and who will be there when I can't sleep? Also, how can I be there for him when he is so far away. We have leaned on each other for over a year already."

"What do you think will happen when he moves?"

"I'm scared we will lose touch and will not talk as much."

"Okay…" Ms. Franklin was waiting for more.

"I'm scared he…. he will forget about me." The tears streamed down my face. I realized why I was so upset about him leaving. "I feel like people forget me when I'm not around, even my mother when she left me so long with my father. Johnathon is my best friend and when he forgets me, it's like I have no one here. This is not how it was supposed to be; and the way he just told me he was leaving. He never gave me a clue he wanted to go home. It kind of pisses me off he was keeping that from me." I couldn't stop sobbing.

"Is the fear and anger about him leaving or is it about you being alone and having to deal with your emotions without him? Is it the threat of dealing with life without the weed and the alcohol that you both grew to depend on? He is the only one who knows that side of you."

"I don't know… I guess." I was gaining my composure.

"So, I know Johnathon is your friend, but now is your chance to learn to sit in your emotions, learn how to cope, make decisions that will benefit you, and break the unhealthy habits that you and Johnathon have formed together. Now the anger you feel about him not telling you he was leaving, is it possible that he didn't tell you because of your reaction to situations? Maybe he didn't want you to cloud his own judgement with your feelings."

"I guess I can look at it like that." My head hung low. Her words stung, maybe I wasn't such a good friend to

Johnathon, maybe he spent our relationship protecting me and my feelings. I thought therapy was supposed to make me feel better, but I was feeling worse by the moment.

"Leesha, however you look at it, you have to move forward. Go on and find happiness for yourself. You can still stay connected with Johnathon, but he is doing what is best for himself; you do the same."

"Right… I am working on making good decisions for myself. I want this chapter in my life to be all about me. Now, I met Karl who is so sweet to me, and I really like him, but I'm scared to get too attached. We have not defined our relationship yet, but there is talk about the future, like traveling together. For all I know, he could disappoint me too. I like him but can't fully fall for him. I promised to work on myself before becoming emotionally and physically involved with anyone." I hadn't planned on mentioning Karl, but I was hoping Ms. Franklin would tell me how to proceed since she was being painfully straight with me today.

"Is Karl single? Has he expressed what his intentions are?"

"Yes, as far as I know he is just seeing me. He hasn't said exactly what his intentions are, but I feel he wants more than just dating."

"Okay. Do you think you can trust yourself to let this man around and still take care of yourself; make you the priority?"

"I think so." *What did she expect me to say, that I'm afraid of becoming some emotionally unstable psycho Bitch; that this man has already dick whipped me and almost swept me off my feet.* I didn't want to hear her mouth about that.

"Good. Earlier you mentioned that you feel like your mother forgot about you when you went to live with your father. We have been talking about the need for you to have that conversation with her. A lot of your fears and relationship habits circle back to what happened with both of your parents. I think your mom can help give you a little clarity on some things. Consider having that talk with her very soon. Maybe you can go visit, get away for a bit. Get her perspective on what happened when you were younger. Maybe you won't be so reluctant to form true bonds and be so fearful of bonds being broken. Consider asking about Leanna, your half-sister." Ms. Franklin gave a weak smile. I knew I drained this lady every time I came.

"I guess that conversation is overdue." I half-heartedly agreed.

Ms. Franklin had mentioned my half-sister, Leanna. That was an extremely touchy subject for me. She was some-one I wanted to talk to, apologize to, hug, and love. I cried every time I thought of how we parted. I was a child, but I just couldn't forgive myself for running out and literally never looking back. That little girl haunted me, I needed to fix that too. I was afraid to find her because I knew she had to hate me for everything that happened, including our dad's death.

After my appointment, I met Mikayla at the mall. She was my first friend I made when I moved to San Antonio. We were both nurses on the same unit and left that job at the same time. She was my go-to when I wanted to do "girl things" like shop for hours or sit at a restaurant with a knowingly long wait. Men, straight or not, were not good for those things. So, when I had to go find some shoes for this event, I called her. I didn't know if women who went to black-tie charity events shopped at the mall, but my shoes will be mall bought. I had ordered a black dress with red accents. According to Johnathon, those were my colors.

While I waited in the car for Mikayla to arrive, I took a deep breath and dialed my mother's number. She answered on the fifth ring.

"Hey, Mom, what are you doing?"

"Hey, Leesha! I'm baking James some fish and veggies. What are you doing?"

"I'm getting ready to go shopping. I just wanted to give you a call."

"What's wrong?" Her voice softened. "I know that voice. You got something to tell me?"

"Yes," I choked the words out. "I'm coming to visit, and I wanted to know if it was okay to come in two weeks, that's all."

"You can come whenever you want, and I know that's not all. But I won't push. I can't wait to see you." Her voice was still soft. That was her way of letting me know I could just say what I needed to now.

"Me too." I didn't take her bait. "I got to go; I think Mikayla just drove up. She's gonna go shopping with me." I ended the conversation.

When we hung up, I took a deep breath and closed my eyes. *I can't believe I'm going to really do this.* Ten minutes later, Mikayla arrived.

"Hey stranger!" She was happy to see me.

"Hey! Thanks for meeting me. I hate shopping alone."

"Sure, you know I'm always ready to shop. What's the occasion again?" she probed.

Here we go. Now I had to tell her about Karl. Of course, she joked saying, "Girl, you better get pregnant and sit down somewhere!" That was just her way of expressing her happiness for me.

We shopped for about three hours and settled in at Kona Grill for an early dinner. I had chosen a pair of black strappy stilettos. I made sure the bottoms were black and not that ugly cheap tan color. That is the best I could do to compete with all the Red Bottoms that would surely be there. I was happy with my choice and knew Francine would like them too.

Francine and I had become pretty close. I showed her a picture of my dress that was to arrive the day before the event. She said I was cutting it too close and suggested I paid the extra to get two-day shipping. She also suggested I go to her seamstress and get my split higher, saying I shouldn't let my beautiful shapely legs go to waste. Francine was so excited for me. She said when I walked in, those "stuffy bitches" were going to be so threatened by me and the men would dream of making love to me. Francine was a wild one, but I liked the way she thought. Like Johnathon she suggested "slut red" lipstick. She said, "make them boring whores as jealous as you can. It's your day, dear. Your show, your stage. Perform darling!" She was becoming my biggest cheerleader.

When I got home, a box was at my front door. I knew it was my dress. I scooped it up and knocked on Johnathon's door. He answered, looking better than he had been in a while. He smiled and opened the door wider welcoming me in. His apartment was down to the bare minimum now, boxes lined the back wall. I felt a little anxious but decided to be a better friend and act happy for him.

"I see you're making progress, that's good." I lied.

He looked at me strangely. "Yea, one more week and I'm out of here. What's in the box?"

"I think it's my dress." I started to open it. After another box, plastic, and tissue paper I held up the dress. "Oh shit, does it look a little small for me?"

"I don't think so. There is only one way to tell; hurry up and put it on." He was genuinely excited for me, not like me with the fake happiness I tried on him moments ago.

I hurriedly pulled off my jeans and shirt. Johnathon watched me intently. He had a look I had never seen before, but I blew it off. I slipped the dress on, thanking God for the stretch it had. I walked to his room to look in his full-length mirror. I looked really good. He stood behind me in the mirror and we both stared at each other. He finally broke the silence.

"You look beautiful. This is the perfect dress for you, thanks to me." He was known to take credit for just about everything.

I smiled. "See, that's why you can't..." I didn't say it. He wrapped his arms around my waist and buried his face in the side of my neck. We just stood there with too many emotions to describe. The atmosphere between us had been so strange. Everything felt so final. I knew it was my mind intensifying every single fleeting thought. That's what therapy was for.

He finally looked in the mirror again. "I am going to miss you, friend."

"I'm going to miss you too, friend. I hope you're happy back home." My smile couldn't mask my sadness.

He leaned down and kissed my cheek. "Can you spend the night with me? Just one last time?" he asked.

I froze in shock, scared knowing it was the worst thing I could do. Wait, Johnathon and I had spent many nights together and it was just like a sleepover with a girlfriend. Maybe he just wanted to spend as much time with me as he could before he left. Okay, who was I fooling, I knew exactly what he was saying, I could tell by the look in his eyes. So, the choices were, stay true to myself and keep pushing toward what I knew I needed, or do something that would feel emotionally and physically good with someone I'm safe with. Either way, my heart would ache when he left.

"I cannot stay with you tonight; my heart can't take that. It's already too hard to let you go."

"Lee, just let me hold you. Just lay with me." He sounded desperate and that wasn't like him. The rare times we were "together" were just substance induced impulses. They were days in which one of us was hurting so much for whatever reason. This was when I realized that Johnathon was just as bad for me as he was good. But I loved this person, I loved the times we had.

"Now, who's being emotional and dramatic?" I tried to lighten the heaviness in the room.

He backed up. "You are correct. I am getting all mushy on you. You better go get this beautiful dress hung up and ready for the big night." He smiled and hung his head.

"Yea, I better go." I pulled up the bottom of my dress, grabbed my clothes, and left. I felt Johnathon's eyes on me as I shut the door.

I got home, carefully removed my dress, laid across my bed, put my hand over my mouth, and sobbed. *It isn't fair how he asked me that, knowing my fragile emotional state. Why? Is he trying to break me more than I already was?* I wanted to grab a bottle of wine and just drink it all and pass out. But that would be the old Lee move. *I'll just get one glass of wine, maybe two.* It was a waste to open a whole bottle and have just one glass.

Later that night, I had one of my nightmares. The thud of the empty wine bottle falling to the floor woke me up. I ran to the restroom, flicked on the light to splash cold water on my face. As I steadied myself on the sink, faint voices next door caught my attention. Johnathon was watching television. I wasn't going back to sleep, so I put on my pajama pants and t-shirt and went next door.

He opened the door as if he expected me to come back. I walked in, and the room was illuminated by the television. He laid on the couch and lifted his blanket, inviting me in. I laid down and he held me until I fell asleep.

CHAPTER 12

Exposed

The next week was hectic but fun. I had my dress altered and my split stopped a few inches below my panties. I mean my left thigh was on full display and I liked it. Francine loved it. Johnathon and Francine finally met, and it was a crazy fun time with both of them. He and I spent the remainder of his days in San Antonio going to all our favorite restaurants and just having a fantastic time. Karl was out of town on business so there was no competition for my time.

The day Johnathon left wasn't as bad as I thought it would be. I promised to come visit in a few months when he got settled. His older sister flew from Arkansas to help him drive back. She looked sad when we said goodbye. We were so close everyone could see how difficult this was for both of us. Karl was there and he promised Johnathon he would take care of me. He was so understanding about Johnathon and knew how important that was to me. Now I could spend some time with him.

The event was the next day. I was excited and had everything planned and laid out. Karl and I went out for lunch, and he finally showed me where he lived. He had a huge home in Cibolo, just outside of San Antonio. When he turned his truck into a long winding driveway, I was already impressed. The deer on his property stopped, watched us get out the truck, and walk to the door. We entered a long corridor decorated with family photos with cowboy stuff mixed in. He threw his keys on a table that had a few rodeo trophies on top and huge random antlers underneath. *This is truly some white boy shit here,* I thought. Other than the hunting décor, it was a beautiful home.

"Karl, this is beautiful! Why would you want to hang out at my place all the time?"

"I really like the land and had this house built. It's more of an investment for me. I don't intend on living here forever."

"This is a nice family home, look at this huge table." My hand glided over a long shiny wooden table with matching chairs.

"I have family gatherings here every now and then. This is the small house for them, but we have a good time here."

"Nice place to entertain the ladies too." I was getting nosey.

"Actually, I really don't bring women here. I don't like people to know where I live."

"Oh, so I'm special?"

"Of course you are."

I walked around his home being nosey. "How many rooms do you have?"

"Five, the master is downstairs and is pretty big, and the others are upstairs."

"Wow." I entered the kitchen, which looked like it came out of a magazine. "You don't cook much, do you? Everything looks new. I'm embarrassed about my small apartment after seeing this."

"No, I don't really cook. I order in or go out. But I like your place, so don't be embarrassed. It's comfortable and intimate." He was moving closer, and my heart flipped. He still made me nervous.

"I missed you, Lee."

He leaned down and gave me a sensual kiss, caressing my face, hair, and arms. I started to feel at ease and melted into him as he licked my neck and came back to my lips. My body grew warm, and my panties became wet. I hadn't experienced that feeling in a while. I felt him swell through my short, blue halter dress. He took my hair down and the thick coils fell to my shoulders. He gently pulled my hair and kissed then licked the other side of my neck. My eyes closed in relaxation, almost like I was just beyond tipsy. My breathing became deep, turning into little gasps as he pulled my halter down exposing my strapless bra. He stopped for a second, making sure he had permission, then blessed my breasts with the same attention he gave my neck. My pussy was painfully wet now as he slowly put his hand under my dress, squeezing my ass through my lace boy shorts. By now his kitchen island was holding most of my weight as I leaned back.

"Let's go to my room," he whispered.

He led me to his room and laid me on his bed. He took his shirt off and I made a silent promise to myself not to go too far. But Karl was so sexy and gentle, like he said before; I was safe with him. It wasn't him I was worried about, it was me. He laid me in the middle of his bed. I was scolding myself, but my body pleaded with me to let whatever was going to happen, just happen. I felt his fingers navigate to my center. Grateful I kept up my waxing appointments, I allowed his fingers to explore. When he felt my smooth, wet pussy he was the one gasping now. As he slowly moved his fingers in and out of me, my lower stomach started tightening. My body slightly trembled as he slid his fingers out, brought them to his mouth and tasted my essence. His eyes locked with mine as he kissed me, letting his tongue play in my mouth, and I desperately kissed him back. He pulled my panties off, kissed, licked, and nipped at my breasts. My moans became louder, and he responded by sliding down my body and eagerly devouring my pussy. He licked and sucked until I moaned louder and rolled my pussy on his face as my hands gripped his head. I was about to lose all control and started scooting away from him.

I pleaded with him to stop but he held me tight almost begging for me to finish on his face. Then there it was, I felt my pussy pulse followed by a creamy wetness that slid down my ass. He wasn't done and slid his fingers in my now dripping pussy and started licking me clean.

When he finished and stood up, that dick was on rock. I got on my knees and crawled to the edge of the bed where he stood and took him into my mouth.

"Oh fuck," he groaned.

I moved back inviting him to the bed. When he got in, I continued to please him with my mouth, returning the favor of course. I took him in deeply, and my gag seemed to turn him all the way on. I did a cough and withdrew him from my mouth letting his pre-cum and my saliva drip from my lips, moistening him before taking him back in. He gripped my hair almost trying to force his whole dick in, I pulled back a bit and he caught control, but his groans were louder as he began to slowly slide my mouth up and down his dick.

His cell phone started ringing, which he ignored. It stopped and started repeatedly, until there was no way for me to ignore it.

"Get that, baby." I backed off.

"Fuck!" He sat up irritated and snatched the phone up. "This is Karl."

"Karl, dammit, what took you so long to answer me?" There was a hysterical woman on the other end.

"I was busy, why are you yelling, Katherine?"

"It's Friday, you're too busy to answer your phone?" She countered.

I got up and Karl slid to the edge of the bed, pulling my arm, and stopping me from walking away. He started stroking his dick as if he were begging me to finish. I kissed his lips, then slid down between his legs to finish him off. He took a deep breath as I took it slowly, waiting for him to end the call.

"Grandmother fell and the facility has called me. I tried to call the manager girl in her office, but of course no answer. That figures." Karl immediately took the phone off speaker. I can only imagine what she was saying about me.

"Was she hurt?" he weakly asked. "Okay, let me call you right back." He hung up the phone and gasped. "Oh fuck." He grabbed my arms, and positioned himself on top of me, entering with urgency and passion. I gripped his soft brown comforter as he rocked me to bliss. His dick pulsated in my pussy, making me crave each stroke and react in desperation for the ultimate orgasm that lingered. I came, and he erupted in pleasure shortly after. He fell back on the bed, breathing heavily with his eyes closed, his whole body was relaxed, and he appeared to be drifting to sleep.

"Where is the bathroom?" I asked. He pointed to a discrete corner.

I went to the bathroom, which was decorated with a big heavy mirror and maroon and black accents. I did what I could to fix myself up and walked out.

He was sitting on his bed and stood up when I came back. He looked at me apologetically.

"Grandmother fell. No one wants to say that she has probably been drinking, but I need to go check on her."

"Okay, can you take me home first? I need to get out these clothes."

"You look great. Go with me. I'm coming right back." He disappeared into the bathroom.

I really wanted to shower. I avoided eye contact when he came out.

"Karl, I really don't mean to be inconsiderate, but I really want to shower, so, I need to go home."

He looked at me and then looked toward the bathroom. He wasn't getting it.

"Okay then, let's shower." He walked toward the large, marbled room, pulling his shirt back off.

Oh no, I thought. I didn't do showers with men. I was in touch with my sexuality and accepted my full size, but still not completely confident. To be honest, I knew Karl was accustomed to those paper-thin women. I had done an extensive social media investigation. Not one woman he had a picture with looked like or was shaped like me. My stomach was flat when I laid down. The thighs are open in the bed, but standing up, there was no hope of a thigh gap. I just stood in the middle of his room, trying to get out of this. Then he pulled the door open, standing with his boxer briefs on and looking at me. I walked slowly to the bathroom and started to take my dress off. He stared at me, watching my every move, and sensed my discomfort.

"You're fine," he reassured me and leaned over to turn the water on. I stepped into the warm shower and grabbed a towel and soap that was placed on the shelf. I quickly started to wash with the intention of getting out as soon as possible.

I heard the curtains open and close behind me and glanced back only to see Karl getting in the shower too.

"Let's hurry, we don't want to keep Francine waiting," I insisted.

"It's okay, she didn't have to go to the hospital. My sister is just overreacting."

He grabbed the soap and towel from me and squeezed soapy water down my body, taking over my shower. It felt good, and I didn't care if the moisture ruined my hair. I leaned against him and took a deep breath as he washed my body. This man had a way of relaxing me. I've never had a man who just wanted to take care of and think about me before himself. My heart felt happy.

When the shower was over, all I wanted to do was lay in his bed and go to sleep. I put my clothes on and brushed my hair back hoping it would dry halfway decently. Karl got dressed and sat on the bed. I knew he felt just as tired and relaxed as I did.

"We better go," I prompted. He sighed and walked toward the door.

When we got to the facility, many of the employees gave me a questioning look. I politely spoke to everyone and continued to Francine's room. When we got there, Francine was lying in bed and Katherine was sitting next to her. Her husband sat across the room, waiting to leave. She glared at me and Karl. His hair was mostly dry, mine was still wet, hanging loosely.

"Well, either you two have been swimming, or you've been screwing. Whichever it is, obviously it was more important than Grandmother." She really got on my nerves.

"Shut up, I'm fine." Francine was clearly irritated. "Come here, my dear." She motioned toward me.

Katherine scoffed and got up. I went to Francine's bedside.

"What happened? How did you fall?" I asked.

"Well, you look refreshed," she said with a smile and wink. "Anyway, I tripped, I didn't fall. Everyone is blowing this out of proportion. This is so silly." She rolled her eyes. "I've been checked, and I am fine. I want to rest and want you all to leave. You didn't have to come in the first place." She was clearly irritated with all the attention.

"Oh God, Grandmother, I'm leaving, since you keep saying that to me." Katherine snatched up her purse, signaled to her husband, and started to walk out. "Karl, can I see you for a minute?" They both followed her.

Francine looked at me. "Well, how are things going with you and Karl?"

"I think we are good." I tried to sound nonchalant.

"Karl has always been full of passion, nothing like his grandfather. He is passionate in his work, his family, and he will be passionate with the love of his life; if you know what I mean." She winked at me. I buried my face in my hands to hide my blushing.

"I don't know what will become of us, but I really like him. I feel so different with him."

"I know the feeling." Her smile let me know that she really knew how I felt, like she had experienced it before. "You better go continue with your day," she insisted.

"Okay, I'm glad you didn't get hurt. See you later, Francine." I gave her a hug.

When I left her room and entered the hallway, I heard Katherine speaking in a scolding tone to Karl.

"So, is that who you were in such a hurry to get to the other day? Wow, Gina has you all messed up, now you're just taking anything! What are you doing with her? Surely you can't be serious about that girl! Gina has been asking about you, she wants to accompany you to the event. My advice is for you to call Gina. Don't be ridiculous!"

"Anything?! What's your damn problem? Gina has nothing to do with who I'm with and Leesha is coming with me to the event, so just leave it alone please." Karl was clearly frustrated.

"Let's go, you're making everything worse, this is ridic-ulous," said the husband. I've never heard him speak. But he was just as annoyed as Karl.

I stood there in the hallway listening. I couldn't say I was surprised, but she was bold to say all that; knowing I was so close. Everyone stopped bickering and turned my way. I looked at Katherine, then decided to save my breath because if I started talking it wouldn't have been a pretty sight. I walked through the middle of their little family huddle, looking in Karl's eyes.

"I'm going to wait in the truck, seems you have some family business to deal with." Karl just shook his head.

I got to the truck, pulled on the door handle, and of course it was locked. Not wanting to wait there like a puppy and risk giving the staff something to talk about, I grabbed my office keys out of my purse and headed back in. Karl was walking my way and he stopped me.

"Where are you going? Come on let's go." His face was tense.

I willingly walked toward the truck to avoid a scene. He opened the door, and my heart raced as I got in. *What am I doing? I shouldn't waste my time because I would never be accepted in this family.*

"Take me home please." I requested as soon as he got in. He hung his head down, then looked at me and touched my leg as if he wanted to say something. "No, just take me home please," my voice was getting shaky.

"Can you please just let me explain what you heard?"

"What I heard? No, what about what I didn't hear?" I was borderline pissed now.

"She just wants me to continue seeing her friend, but that was a long time ago. Katherine has issues."

"Will she be there tomorrow?"

"Yes, of course. Why?"

"I am not sure I want to be around her or that whole scene of people looking for your ex and seeing me."

"What difference does it fucking make? I want you there."

"Just take me home."

"Why are you being like this? My feelings for you are what matters, nothing else." He was so sincere. That scared the shit out of me, but what scared me more was falling for someone whose family wouldn't accept me, like my mother did.

"Everything else matters, Karl! I can't become part of this mess." Tears stung my eyes. "I'm trying to stay whole! Don't you see? I can't give you a piece of my heart and have you just take it and leave. I'm not strong enough to recover from something like that. I need to make good decisions and pay attention to what I see, not what I feel. Emotions get me in trouble." I was full-blown crying by now.

"Lee, I am not going to leave. The only way we will part is if you want to, not me."

"You say that, but eventually you will have some decisions to make involving your family and me. Eventually you'll have to choose, and when people have decisions to make and I'm involved, I lose! I'm the one always left alone. When things get rough, I'm the one sacrificed. I can't be that person again." My tears were persistent, everything was spilling out at once.

"Just let me prove it to you, let me prove I will not hurt you." Karl hung his head, looking defeated. "You will not lose with me, and I gave you my heart a long time ago. You are scared, so am I, but choose to be with you, regardless of you pushing me away; please believe me." Karl was holding my face, forcing me to look at him.

"Please, take me home," were the only words that came out.

"Not until you say you believe me," he insisted.

"I'm trying to believe you, but give me a minute, please." I was so upset.

During the ride home, I didn't say a word. I sat there silently, looking out the window fighting the tears. That battle was lost, and the tears flowed, physically and emotionally exposing the ache and disappointment I felt. There was my answer to "why me?" I was a rebound, a jump off. He probably wanted to take me to this event to shock his fucking lame ass friends and family. Not to mention, to make this Gina chick jealous. Fuck this.

CHAPTER 13

Go and Show

As soon as I got to my floor, my instinct was to knock on Johnathon's door. But I remembered Johnathon had been my latest loss. He chose his family who didn't accept him over our friendship. I felt myself losing ground. Irrational thoughts took over. I shouldn't have broken the promise to stay out of any type of relationship until I could handle the consequences, good or bad. I got in my apartment, laid on the couch, and tried consoling myself. Johnathon was on the road, and I hated bothering him, but I did, and called, telling him all about the day, and how I wasn't going to that stupid event.

"Leesha, that is all the more reason to go to the event. Let them mother fuckers hate on you. Fuck his sister and that ex. Go and show."

"I don't need to waste my time with it. This whole scene won't benefit me at all."

"Just go, have fun, forget about anything long term, just put on that dress you paid for and go. After it's over you can decide if you still want to mess with Karl. But he likes you and it's not his fault his sister is crazy and wants him with someone else, that's her deal."

"You're right. I paid for my dress already. I'll go, and probably leave Karl alone afterwards. If I deal with someone, I don't want to worry about having his family working against me."

"Whatever Lee, you trying to be with Karl, not the whole damn family. Just think about that before you put that man down. I gotta go, we're stopping at the store. Call me after the event; I want details."

"Okay Johnathon, talk to you later, love you."

"Love you too, Lee."

He was right. When I got off the phone, I felt better, and decided to start getting myself together. I called Lisa, the lady that did my hair, and made an appointment. My nails and toes were getting done today too. I called the MAC store and made an appointment to get my make-up done tomorrow. This was the perfect way to treat myself.

After getting home from my appointment, Karl called, and we spoke for a few minutes. It was awkward, but he sounded relieved that I was still going. I put some rollers in my hair to maintain the style, went to bed, and slept well.

I woke up early and decided to watch Lifetime and chill for the day before getting ready. I ate light and decided against my usual pregame cocktail. Later, I went to my make-up appointment.

"Something bold with red lipstick," I told the guy preparing to do my face.

He studied me and asked about the event. "No, let's smoke your eyes out and give you a glossy nude lip. It will accent your light brown eyes and golden-brown skin," he insisted.

"Okay," I agreed.

I was excited and pleased with the way everything was coming together but was sure to keep in mind that I was just going to this event because Johnathon did a good job of convincing me, and the safest thing to do was to leave Karl alone after this. I was an educated woman, made good money, and would be okay without him. Attaching myself to a man with a family that made me feel less than worthy was a mistake. But that night, I planned on having a nice evening, drinking responsibly, eating, and talking shit about people in my mind.

When my make-up was done, the artist turned me toward the mirror, stepped back, and waited for my reaction.

"Oh my God. I don't even recognize myself." He'd placed some eyelashes on to extend my already full ones. The black, brown, and gray shadow he used highlighted the gold and green specks in my brown eyes. My cheekbones were dusted with pale pink, lips were a glossy pinkish nude color, and a light bronzer was applied in selected areas. I brought some of the products he used, promised to post pics on my page, and tag him. I wasn't a big social media person, but this warranted a post.

I started getting ready as soon as I got home. It was a challenge squeezing into my Spanx and I thought about wearing some shear panty hose, but decided against it because my thighs were firm enough to pull this off. I mixed my rose oil and shimmer lotion to rub on my legs, arms, and chest. I carefully slipped on my dress, now realizing that the high slit made me feel self-conscious, but it was too late to get bashful now. I lightly brushed the right side of my hair. It was blown out and loosely curled. Some of the curls almost covered my eye. The left side of my hair was held back with tight twists that were just edgy enough to match the split in my dress. My tattoo on my thigh looked extra sharp thanks to the oil. It was 7:00 p.m. and Karl was supposed to pick me up at 7:15. The cocktail hour was supposed to start at 7:30. The place that the event was being held at was thirty minutes away. I liked the fact that we were going to be a little late so we would make an entrance.

I took a few selfies and posted them. Right away there was a heart emoji. My heart fell to my stomach when Mike's name popped up. Oh no, not the reaction I needed right now. I closed my eyes and took a deep breath and by the time I opened them, there was a message.

"I've never been ghosted so bad in my life. I miss you so much. How are you?"

The message made me nervous, and my gut warned against me responding.

"I'm good." The immediate response exposed my weakness for him.

"When can I see you? We can have coffee."

"No, I'm good," I decided to cut it short now.

"I'm not good, but whatever." I could tell he was salty as fuck.

I didn't respond this time, but there was another message alert. Holy shit, the devil was busy this evening. It was Roy. The message said nothing, but my screen displayed a pic of him naked as far as I could tell, it stopped right before exposing his dick. He looked sexy as fuck; that young freak thought all he had to do was show his body. I couldn't say he was completely wrong. I responded with the eye roll emoji. He responded with a heart and *"I miss you, babe."* Although it was tempting, he was left on read too.

There was a knock at my door, and I took another glance in the mirror. *Okay, here goes nothing.* I opened the door and there stood Karl, looking sharp. His eyes widened as he studied me.

"Lee, you look stunning. I'm going to be the luckiest man in the room."

"Thank you. You look nice too." I grabbed my clutch off the table, and we headed out.

When we got to the car, the driver was standing outside. He was a tall, good-looking Black man and by the way he peered at me, it was obvious he liked what he saw too. I gave him a secret side smile as he opened the door, and I slid in. He returned with a slight smile and a sly wink. *I'm such an attention whore,* I thought to myself. Karl was none the wiser as he answered his cell phone, sliding in beside me.

Karl said his goodbyes to whomever he was talking to and refocused on me. He grabbed my hand and gave me a kiss. "I'm so glad you still decided to come tonight. I know what you heard was upsetting, but Katherine does not speak for me, and you know I love being with you. I would like to see you more. I want us to get closer if you will allow it." His eyes sparkled.

He was already making me weak. "I know, Karl. I believe I have a lot to offer and for your sister to refer to me as 'just anything' was so demeaning. Who is Gina by the way?" When I asked that question, I saw the driver quickly look at us through the mirror. He had the 'it's going down' look.

"Gina is my ex. Not really an ex, we were never serious. My sister liked her more than I did."

"Okay you were never serious, but was she? Not that it's any of my business, but if this is going to be a competition between me and an ex, I don't need it." I had to be honest.

"There is and will be no competition. Give me a chance to prove to you how much I like you and how much I want to be with you, only you." His eyes were genuine.

Karl told me before that he liked me because I was more independent than he was accustomed to. He said that needy women stressed him out. Of course, he was interested in seeing where this relationship would go emotionally and physically. If he had met me months before, it wouldn't have worked because I was unsure and needy. God's timing had done us right in that regard.

I felt the driver looking at us. I bet he could've given me the real scoop on what was going on with this family. I glanced at the driver, catching Karl's attention. His eye did a quick pivot from the driver then to me.

"I don't want to get into a heavy conversation. Let's just go with the flow tonight." I gave him a kiss to divert his attention from the fact he caught me peeking at the driver.

When we got to the event, the driver opened the door, and I made it a point not to look his way. I knew Karl was on alert now. How funny, he probably had at least ten women there that he had fucked, and now wants to guard me. I reminded myself that I was just coming here tonight, but was in self-preservation mode, this meant that guards were up, and the red flags were waving.

When we walked in, the room was brighter than I thought it would be. The tables were decorated with black tablecloths, vases filled with white roses, and had candles placed in small crystal votives. Accents of shiny silver stones were strategically placed around the votives and vase. It was beautiful. I looked around the room and noticed we caught a few eyes. But what I was really searching for is that hag

Karl called a sister. Karl took my arm and guided me to the dreaded table that his sister and her husband were sitting at. I paused and he turned toward me.

"You're good, she will behave, she doesn't show her real self in public, especially at this event," he reassured me. I thought it was disrespectful that he had me sit with her but was sure the seating was already pre-arranged. That's okay, I would just sit there and behave as well.

As the night progressed, I was aware that plenty of eyes were on me, being one of only three Black people there. After dinner, Karl and I walked around, and he introduced me to several colleagues and some friends that were scattered through the crowd. Karl made it a point to either hold my arm or hand. As we walked around, the men Karl didn't acknowledge made no secret of eyeing my leg that presented itself through the exaggerated split in my black, curve hugging gown. The inside was lined with a deep red that also outlined my cleavage area. Don't get me wrong, Karl attracted just as much attention as I did. He was a beautiful, tall man, and those eyes made me want to hold onto him just as much as he held onto me.

I had to excuse myself and go to the restroom. I dreaded wrestling with my spanks, but I'd held off as long as possible. The restroom was beautiful with a seating area and other amenities. I took my time because I really did need a break from all the fake mingling we were doing. I was washing my hands at the sink when a nice looking, slender red head stood next to me to wash hers.

"I come to this event every year, never seen you here before." She smiled and eyed me.

"It's my first time. This is nice." I returned the smile.

"I see you're with Mr. Michaels."

"Yes."

"Yea, he and I go way back." She turned toward me.

"Oh, really. He didn't introduce me to you." I already knew where this shit was heading.

"I didn't think he would." She gave a half grin. "Nice meeting you." She left before I could say anything more.

When I walked out, I looked around for Karl. I walked through the crowd for about fifteen minutes before giving up and going back to the table. Katherine and her husband were still sitting there chatting with another couple. The other gentleman jumped up and pulled out the chair for me as he burned a hole through my dress. I was happy to oblige because if he had to go home with that overly thin basic bitch he was with; he needed some inspiration. His seat was right across from mine. He sat down and proceeded to stare at my breasts. Okay, he was a bit much now. I turned to the side to look at the crowd and to stop him from staring at me.

After about twenty minutes, Katherine got my attention and asked, "are you looking for Karl?" She turned toward a discreet hallway and nodded her head. I followed her gaze and spotted Karl talking to the red head in the corner. The conversation looked heated. She was in his face saying something. She started to walk off and he grabbed her arm.

She turned back around and covered her face and fell into his chest as if she were crying. He held her.

By this time, Katherine was staring at me with a smirk on her face. This whole scene was too much, I wasn't going to be played in front of all these people. I got up and walked over there. Karl looked up before I made it to him. He let her go and stepped to the side. I stepped right in their face and silently dared that bitch to say something, and the same with him.

"I am leaving. I've had enough." I said, giving him an attitude, he had never seen.

"Lee, this is not what it looks like," he protested while grabbing my arm.

"Oh, what does it look like? Does it look like you are having a fight with your bitch while I sit there watching? Is that what it looks like?" I spoke in a quiet voice. His face filled with shock and disappointment; I knew he never had anyone charge him up like that. I turned and looked at Ms. Red, crossed my arms, and let her know she had better leave. Her eyes darted back and forth between me and Karl, then she walked off.

"Leesha, can I please talk to you. You know I wouldn't do anything like that," he said in a voice just as intimidating as mine. Then he softened up. "You know I like you. That was Gina. There wasn't anything serious between us, I don't fucking know why she is acting like this."

I turned around and walked toward the door and he followed. I got outside and looked around for the car. The driver was standing by another car, smoking, and talking to an older man. He saw me, threw his cigarette on the ground, and stepped on it as he walked toward me.

"Take me home," I said with tears welling in my eyes. He nodded and opened the door. Just as the door opened, I heard Karl's voice.

"I got it," he told the driver as he grabbed the door. I avoided looking at him.

"Please don't go, I have to stay for the presentation, and want you here…I need you here, just stay." Karl begged.

"I've been humiliated enough, Karl." I was more sad than anything.

With a defeated look, he backed away, shut the door, and hit the top of the car giving the driver a signal to go.

CHAPTER 14

The Relapse

The driver was quiet the first ten minutes of the ride. He glanced at me several times, and I stared out the window, embarrassed. He probably was thinking "this Black chick had no business with this dude," I assumed.

"You look beautiful tonight," he finally broke the awkward silence between us.

"Thank you." I was so choked up and could barely get the words out.

"I don't know what happened in there, I could only imagine, but I can tell you that he really likes you. He's been getting ready all day for this. I've been driving him for 2 years and never seen him so happy. When I saw you, I could see why."

"Yea?" I looked at him. "Seems like he and his red head girlfriend were having a lover's quarrel. Meanwhile I was sitting there looking ridiculous."

"There's nothing ridiculous about you. Where do you work?" he asked.

"I'm a supervisor at the facility where his grandmother lives."

"Ms. Francine! I love her. She's the coolest person in that family."

"Agreed," I chuckled.

We small-talked the whole way home. I learned he was going to college, engaged to his girlfriend of six years, and wanted to have a big family. We talked about crazy moments he had with Francine, like driving her to the liquor store on the "bad" side of town so she wouldn't run into anyone she knew. According to him, she was cool with the men that hung around the liquor store. That was so funny, but that definitely sounded like Francine.

When I got home, he made me promise to talk to Karl. I agreed to call him but didn't mean it. Karl and I were a done deal. I got to my apartment and automatically knocked on Johnathon's door. This night was getting worse. The heels and dress were off, and Spanks were gone as soon as I got through the door. My phone chimed with another message from Mike, which was the last thing I needed.

I didn't respond. Instead, I went to the fridge and pulled out a bottle of wine, grabbed some Patrón out of the cabinet, took a shot, then poured me a glass of wine. As I was getting ready to sit down, I spotted the small, mirrored box that Johnathon had left me. *What the hell,* I thought; opened it, pulled out the bag of weed and papers, rolled a joint, and went out to my balcony to sit and enjoy the rest of the night. I smoked and drank, hoping I would just pass out. My phone rang and I answered without looking at the ID, kind of hoping it was Karl.

"Hello." Hearing Mike's voice made my heart pound. *Shit! I shouldn't have answered.*

"Why are you calling me? Is your wife sleep or something?"

"I didn't call to answer questions about my wife. I called to hear your voice."

"Well, you heard my voice, so we can say bye."

"Leesha! Don't fucking hang up on me. You just up and stopped talking to me and I didn't deserve that shit."

"Mike, you are married. I have the right to just cut you off with no explanation."

"Yes, and you knew that. You also knew that I fucking fell for you, and you were my friend too. I miss you. Can I just come over to talk?"

"It's too late for talking."

"I'm on my way." The phone went dead.

By this time, I could safely say I was high as a kite and drunk as shit. Unfortunately, I was pitiful and now wanted to see him. I went back inside and dozed off.

I woke up to a knock. When I opened the door, there stood Mike in gym pants and a black T-shirt. He looked like he had been working out. "Well looks like you've had a late night at the gym." My speech was a little slurred.

"I had a lot of stress to relieve." He walked toward me and gave me a hug. *Lord why did this have to feel so good, so comforting.* I returned the hug and felt him exhale.

Then the drunken tears started running down my face. "I'm so fucked up," I whimpered. He released his embrace and lifted my chin to see the tears falling. I'm sure my eye make-up was all over my face by now. He wiped my tears.

"What is wrong?" His voice was gentle.

"I'm drunk, high, and my night was terrible. Now you're here and you shouldn't be. Anyway, I went to this function with this guy. He is way out of my league."

"First of all, there is no one out of your league, so stop it," he interrupted me.

"Do you want to hear the story or not? So, we get there, everything is going well, then the minute I leave his side, he is off in some corner fighting, making up, or whatever with his ex. I am sitting there, feeling like everyone is staring at me, humiliated, ashamed. He probably only took me to make her jealous."

"Well, you got this all figured out, don't you? Lee, that is a story you are making up in your head. Don't get me wrong, lucky for me, he did fuck up tonight, but you have a way of always putting yourself down, making yourself the underdog in every scenario. I don't want that for you. I want you to know your worth. I want you to realize whoever is with you is crazy about you. You need to be crazy about yourself too." I'd never seen him so serious.

He was right. But that is what I was working on when I let everything go, including him, Roy, drinking, smoking, overeating, all that shit. I was doing good. Then I met Karl, then Johnathon left me, then I let Mike in my presence. I was weak, mentally weak.

We sat in silence, listening to our mix of music. Luther Vandross' *Superstar* came on. Mike reached over and pulled me closer to him. I snuggled into his chest. He held me even closer as I started drifting to sleep.

"You got to go, I'm tired." I weakly insisted.

"Can I lay with you for a while? I miss you so much."

"I don't think you should do that, but whatever." I didn't have much fight in me, so I caved easily.

I felt gross, my face still full of smeared make-up and sweaty. I just wanted to be comfortable after the long day. I took a quick shower, brushed my teeth, took some Tylenol, and drank some cold Gatorade to combat the inevitable morning hangover. When I got to my bed, Mike was there, snoring. I already didn't like men spending the night, now I had to listen to snoring until he woke up and left. I laid down on the other side of the bed and drifted to sleep.

I woke up during the night and caught Mike looking at me. I was hoping he wasn't going to try to have sex, because what he had to offer would send me further down the spiral I was in already.

"Maybe you should go," I suggested.

"I want to stay a little longer."

"Why?"

"Because I missed you and the way you ended things tore me up. I need to do this right."

I just looked at him, somehow knowing this was the end, and so did he.

"I know that we're not together and, in your mind, we never really were, cause…well, because I'm married." His conflicted expression strangely made me want to console him.

"Okay." I touched his face with empathy.

"I just want you to know, I did and do love you. I know that is something we would never say, but I love you and I really need you to know that." He held me close and inhaled deeply as if he was relishing my scent.

"What is this, Mike? What's wrong with you?"

"I just know you're moving on, and I don't want to stop you."

"Okay, Mike." I felt sad but refused to show it this time. I wanted to be mad at myself for even letting him in, but I couldn't. I was glad I saw him. My heart was so heavy, but the weight had been lifted. This was true closure.

CHAPTER 15

Reasons Why

After that night, I didn't have time to worry about what happened with Karl or think about Mike. I now had crazy anxiety about flying out to see my mother in two days. I spent the next day packing and made dinner plans with Mikayla to tell her about the past few days and relax before my trip.

We met at a Mexican restaurant so we could get some good margaritas. I ate light so my stomach wouldn't get upset on the plane the next morning. She was updated on everything that happened with Karl and Mike.

"Damn, your life goes from zero to one hundred in no time. So have you talked to Karl today?"

"No, we probably will talk again, but I'm sure the romance thing is gone. The truth is, I don't really know who fucked it up, me or him. I could've ignored that whole scene with him and the ex, and took him home with me later, but I guess it doesn't matter now."

"When you get back home after everything calms down, you really should call him and don't waste time thinking of Mike. Thank God that shit is over!" She lifted her hands in praise.

"Cheers to that shit being over!" Those were the words that came out of my mouth, but my heart did ache a little. Thinking about Karl made it ache more. He was the one I was supposed to be with, but my mind wouldn't let me. Mikayla reached over and gave my hand a squeeze. I guess the pain on my face was apparent.

"You will be okay, Lee. You always make it out okay."

Her words, *make it out okay.* That meant I was always in some self-sabotaging shit, messing with people I didn't need to, and doing unnecessary shit. That's okay. After this trip to see my mom was over, I was getting it together… again.

I went to bed early to rest for the flight, but my sleep was tense and broken. Around 1:30 a.m. a knock on the door woke me up. I tiptoed to look through the peephole. It was Karl. My heart was pounding as I cracked open the door.

"What are you doing here?" I asked.

"Open the door please," he demanded.

"I got an early flight and was sleeping." I decided on being difficult.

"Don't act like this, I'm here, let me in now." I had never seen that type of aggression from him. I opened the door, allowing him to walk in. *So much for using my good judgement*, I thought.

"Excuse me." I ran to get my robe to cover my neon green boy shorts and tank top. I returned, pausing in the hallway watching him slowly case my living room. His eyes finally landed on me.

"I didn't mean to scare you. You act like I'm a serial killer." The moonlight peeked through my sheer curtains enough to put an eerily dim spotlight on him.

"I'm not a fan of people coming to my house unannounced."

"Oh, so I'm 'just people' now." Karl wasn't only angry, but he was also drunk.

"You have to leave; I was sleeping." My gut was telling me to end this interaction.

"Oh, are you tired? Did you have a long night after you left me, Leesha?"

Oh shit, I knew where this was going. "No Karl, I didn't."

"I came by last night; you didn't answer your door. I came back this morning and saw a man leaving." Karl's watery eyes peered straight into mine.

"Karl, I didn't hear you knock if you did come by and the guy you saw leaving was just a friend, nothing happened, I promise."

"I should believe you, but you never believe me, is that how this goes, Leesha?"

I said nothing, I was so upset with myself, and knew this conversation was going to escalate badly.

"You fuck that man, Lee? After you left me, was he the one you were running to?" Karl's southern accent was stronger than I've ever heard it. He threw his cowboy hat on the couch.

"Karl, no, no, please believe me, baby, I didn't sleep with him." *Since when did I start begging?* I thought. But now suddenly, the tables were turned, and I didn't want to lose Karl, not like this. I gripped his shirt as if it would make him believe me.

He looked into my eyes and suddenly gave me an angry kiss. The liquor on his lips was pungent, causing me to immediately withdraw. He pushed me until my back was against the wall. His sadness and anger flooded my soul, and my tears came as I tried to catch control of his aggressiveness.

His tears fell as we kissed then he whispered in my ear. "Please tell me, I'm not a fool, Lee, please," he begged. I had really hurt him, and was so angry with myself, regardless of what I thought happened at that fundraiser with his ex.

"Karl, no you're not a fool, I promise. Seriously, he came over unexpectedly and we just talked. It got late so he slept on the couch. Nothing happened." I was halfway honest.

I was crammed between the wall and him and his kiss was more urgent now. Everything in me was responding to him as he took complete control of my body. He untied my robe and gripped my breasts, and his lips finally controlled mine. One hand traced down my body, sliding two fingers into the side of my shorts, finding my pussy. I gasped in pleasure, encouraging his passionate aggression, and his kisses traced to my neck and traveled to my breasts, licking and biting. He was being rough, but I liked it. As my knees weakened, he was able to keep me steady against the wall. He licked his fingers, looked in my eyes, and got on his knees.

I was trembling with nerves, like this was new to me. No one had really just manhandled me, much less while I stood up. He lifted my left leg and put it over his shoulder, pulled my now soaked shorts to the side, slowly licked my pussy, and sucked my clit. He fingered me almost to tears, causing unstoppable tingling all the way down to my pussy. I screamed as I unwillingly came, feeling my wetness trickle down my inner thigh followed by his velvet tongue. He stood back up with his hard dick pressing between my legs. He urgently kissed my mouth; his tongue dominating that space too. I was weak, my legs were trembling, and my unsteadiness made him back off.

"Let's go to your room." His voice was low and demanding.

I clumsily led him to the room. My back was still turned when I felt him grab me, kiss my neck, using my hair to bring my head back. His gentle force pushed my body down, and I crawled quickly onto my bed. I heard him removing his clothes and started to turn over.

"No, stay like that," he ordered.

I turned back over to my stomach and heard the tear of a condom wrapper. He crawled on the bed, lifted my hips bringing me to my knees, kissed my neck, moved his tongue down my back, and then gave my pussy some more strokes. I immediately started to cum again. He came back up and entered me, now stroking me with his dick. It was so slow, torturous, and he knew it was making me crazy. I started to moan, wanting to ask him to do it faster and harder.

Finally, he leaned over, whispered in my ear, "What's wrong, baby?"

"Nothing." My voice was a whimpered pant.

"Tell me what you want. Just say what you want, baby. Do you want me to fuck you faster, harder? You want to cum again, baby?"

"Yes, yes please."

He turned me over and cuffed my neck as he entered me again. His strokes were rhythmic and hard. I grabbed my headboard to brace myself as he fucked me. When I started to cum, he squeezed my neck a little harder, making me lightheaded, and we came simultaneously. Feeling like I passed out, I forced my eyes open. *Is this white boy trynna kill me?* I thought. But I felt so damn satisfied. Karl was now dead weight on top of me. He was the one who passed out.

So that was drunk sex with Karl. No, that was angry, hurt, drunk sex with him. I wasn't sure he trusted anything I said. But right then, I just wanted to hold him. He rolled off me and pulled my body against his, like he never wanted to let me go. I curled into him because maybe I was the one who didn't want to let go.

Karl woke me up about 3:15 a.m. with a kiss on the back of my neck and a gentle pull of my hair. He lifted my leg and stroked me from the back. His dick drove me crazy, and I could tell I did the same for him. After that, he said he had to go, and he'd see me later. He was still pissed; I could tell. Maybe he just needed to blow off steam and get me out of his system. I officially felt manipulated and used, from what I now knew as revenge sex.

That morning, I got an Uber to the airport. My flight was at 6 a.m. and I didn't want to get anyone up that early. When I made it through security, I got settled, sat down, and waited to board the plane. I kept looking at my cellphone, hoping Karl would call or text. He didn't.

The flight was short and uneventful. It wasn't full, so I had a row to myself. My thoughts of Karl changed quickly to the upcoming talk with my mother. I thought about all the feelings that it could trigger, and wondered how this would play out. She was so excited about this visit. I wondered how she would take it when I had the long overdue conversation. My stomach ached just thinking about it.

I called Mom as soon as I landed in Louisiana and made it outside with my luggage to wait. As I checked my phone again, I heard a horn blow and there was James' smiling face jumping out of a white BMW. *What a nice car; mom has come a long way.* This was a far cry from her past life. I gave him a hug and handed him my bag. He threw it in the back seat and opened the passenger's side for me.

"You look so good, girl, I tell ya! Me and your momma are so happy you finally got here to see us." James had a thick southern accent.

"I am glad to see you too! How are you doing? I missed you both so much. So, what have you two been up to?"

"Well, since my little heart attack, Lucie got me on the most tasteless diet ever." He sighed. "That's another reason I'm happy you're here. She is frying chicken, making gumbo, rice, and cornbread. Not to mention the German chocolate cake and sweet potato pie!" He sounded so excited. "Lucie said the days you're here I can eat whatever I want."

"Well, lucky you! I'm glad my visit could benefit you." James always had such a good sense of humor.

Their neighborhood was nice and quiet. The houses were beautiful with well-kept yards. We pulled up to the red brick home with stark white accents and a brilliantly green lawn. Mother opened the door and walked toward the car with a huge smile. Her dark brown skin was smooth and obviously well moisturized. Her relaxed hair was pinned up with spiraled curls hanging to one side of her slender face. My mother's father was Creole, and her mother was from the Bahamas. Looking at her face and thin but shapely frame made me wonder how the hell did I get all this body. I jumped out and gave her a big hug and she kissed me with her full heart-shaped lips. She really could've been a model if her life had played out differently, maybe if she hadn't met my father.

My father was the total opposite of James. My mind instantly became consumed with his permanent effect on our lives. He was dead and my mother seemed to be living the perfect life regardless of past events, but I knew she was just as haunted by the past as I was. That discussion would be coming very soon.

That evening, dinner was great. She always cooked everything perfectly. James damn near killed himself eating all that food. She stopped him by taking his third plate away right as he was digging in. He looked sad but conceded to their silent fight.

Later that evening after James went to bed, we sat on the couch to watch a movie, and ended up talking about James' heart attack, his family, and their last family reunion. We went to bed around midnight after making plans for brunch and shopping the next day.

I decided to have the talk during brunch. As I went to one of the guestrooms, my mind was preoccupied with rehearsing that conversation. The room I chose was decorated in black with gold accents. It was sexy but classy, definitely her style. She had live plants everywhere, displaying her green thumb. Some of the rooms were separated with long strands of multicolored beads. She had always done her own thing. Her free, lackadaisical spirit led most of her life's decisions, the decisions that defined so much of my life.

The next morning, I was up and ready early. I spent time sitting at the table drinking coffee and chatting with James. He gleefully helped himself to two pieces of sweet potato pie as we waited for the princess to wake from her beauty sleep. When she finally got up, she took her time getting ready and presented herself in a casual black and white pants outfit. Her hair was pulled back in a high ponytail with spiral curls hanging just past her neck. Her hair had grown, and she looked younger and happier every time I visited. That had a lot to do with the love James showed her and that Louisiana retirement.

We left close to noon to have brunch at a little restaurant that was owned by one of her friends. We had shrimp and grits, a veggie omelet, and fruit. I figured this was as good as time as any to start the discussion. I just wanted answers, so I could heal and allow true love into my life.

"Mom." I reached over and grabbed her hand across the table. She looked up at me with a combination of surprise, fear, and dread on her face. Maybe I was reading too much into her expression, but she looked like she knew what was coming. We were never the touchy- feely mother-daughter duo, so that was her clue something was wrong.

"Yes. What's going on?"

"Mom. I need to talk to you about what happened when I was younger. I am so confused and sad. This is wearing me down and I need you to talk to me about it."

Her eyes started to water. She was a crybaby, just like me. "Okay, about what?"

I was hoping she wasn't going to make this hard, but the "about what" question proved me wrong.

"About why you made me stay with him and his family. About when I was back with you and happy; you went to jail for two years leaving me with the neighbor, of all people. I wasn't a fan of my father, but why was I not allowed at his funeral when none of this was my fault. I got a program in the mail." My voice began to crack. I covered my face, gave myself a silent pep talk, and continued. "No one cared about me and what was happening. I didn't have a permanent home until I was almost in high school. It was too late; I already couldn't make sense of my life." I was tearful by now.

She touched my face. "I always wanted you. I did the best I could. When I took you to your father's house, my intent was to get you in a month. I just needed to get back on my feet. When I got pregnant by your father, his family already hated me because I was Black. He had a girlfriend that I found out about after the fact. Your grandmother was addicted to drugs; she had multiple men in and out of the house to support her habit. Some of those men would try to come into my room. I stayed with my mother as long as I could, till you were five. I left and got a small apartment. That is where we stayed until you were seven." She didn't look at me when she was speaking. It was almost as if she was ashamed.

"I remember that. I remember our little Christmas tree, sleeping with you every night, until that day you took me to his house."

"Well, I guess you don't remember sleeping in the car for two weeks. That is why I took you to him. It was cold out and I didn't want you to suffer with me. I called him and he wasn't thrilled about having you there, but he agreed. I called again before I dropped you off and his wife answered. She seemed nice and said that she had your room ready. She claimed that Leanna was excited to have her big sister stay with her. That conversation made me feel better about leaving you there."

"Mom, he was ashamed of me. I was his Black accidental child. He made me go into the closet as punishment for whatever. The closet was filled with junk, and it just looked scary in there. I would cry and he would bang on the door telling me to shut up. Leanna never got locked in there, so I knew that was just reserved for me. When his parents came over, I had to stay in my room and eat dinner, while they all sat at the table. I heard him tell them I was in my room because I was bad at school or something. He would curse me out when I asked Helen to help me wash my hair. No one knew what to do with it. My teacher would bring stuff to school and help me wash my hair in the sink because it smelled. She would blow dry and French braid it while all the other kids were at recess. Those were just a few things I had to go through there. His wife just stood by and let it happen. She was no better. Leanna would just cry for me. She was the only one that knew it was wrong." By now the tears flooded my face.

"I found out about all of that and came to get you," she stammered with watery eyes.

"How did you find out? I was trapped and just thought my prayers were answered when you showed up."

"Helen found me, and she begged me to get you."

"Helen found you?" That information took me off guard.

"Yes, I was working in a Bar and Grill and still trying to get on my feet. I even went back to your grandmother's house for a while." She looked down and held herself. "I was glad I didn't bring you because her boyfriend was very aggressive. He always came to my room. Of course, I was grown, so most nights I fought him off. But you would've never been able to get away from him."

"Mom, I'm sorry that was happening to you. I had no idea."

"It's okay, I'm still here." She gave an encouraging smile. "Anyway, long story short, Helen found me and gave me the money to rent that house, money for groceries, and for whatever else we needed for a few months. She did all that just so I could come get you. But that was our secret. That is why she always stayed so silent. She didn't want him to get suspicious. He would hit her too."

"He didn't hit me, but he made my life miserable."

"Well, behind closed doors she caught hell too. So, I picked you up and your father was so angry and said he would beat my ass if I ever asked him for anything. But I took you and we were living okay. Later on, my car broke down and I had to buy another one. School was starting for you, and you needed supplies and clothes. I applied for benefits, and they automatically put child support on him. So, of course he got the news and did just what he said he would do. He came to my home and wanted to fight. You were there, don't you remember?"

"Not really. I think that day was so traumatic for me. All I remember was the ambulance and police walking around. I saw very little, because our neighbor, Ms. Sandy, closed the blinds and sent me to the back room. That room ended up being mine for two years. I really didn't even know why. Ms. Sandy was good to me, she raised me with her grand-children. But never talked about how I ended up with her for so long."

"Well, your dad and I had a pretty bad fight. No, it was more like a brutal attack on me. I sent you to your room as soon as he got there, so you didn't see it. When he had me on the ground choking and hitting me, we were right by the couch. I kept a gun under the couch cushions. But when I got to it, he wasn't scared at all. Matter of fact he laughed at me and said 'Bitch, you don't have the fucking guts.' He grabbed me by my hair and pulled me outside. He slammed me on the porch and just started to leave. He just started walking away." She shook her head as if she couldn't believe it. "I stood up, held up the gun and shot him in his back. I guess the shock made him turn to face me, so I shot him in the chest." Mom looked down and then back at me. "I spent two years in jail waiting for my trial, and you spent two years with Sandy. Helen didn't testify for me or against me.

I think she was actually relieved, but she didn't dare show it. I had a public defender, who knew the Mohans well. He worked more against me than for me. Then one day another attorney showed up. But this one was privately paid. I was told an advocate for wrongfully accused African Americans paid him." She looked as if she was hearing this for the first time too. Maybe she never really had to tell this story.

I sat looking at her, more shocked than anything. What I thought to be true wasn't. I've always felt abandoned. My father always told me that no one wanted me, not even my mother because I was a mistake, and I would end up alone like my mom or a junkie like my grandmother.

"My heart ached for you every night. I hated myself for not being there to take care of you. I had you young and thought I was in love with him. He didn't make me believe anything different, until his father found out about me. He was sent away until after you were born. He came back married to Helen."

"You mean he was capable of showing love?"

"Oh, yes. In my mind you were conceived out of love. I don't know what his father did or said to make him flip."

Mom moved closer to me and rubbed my back. I didn't need her to comfort me. I think I was past that. "Lee, I tried to make everything right when I got out of jail. We had some good times too, so don't just keep dwelling on the bad ones. I tried my best to show you I loved you more than anything in the world, I still do. Our lives took a terrible turn, but we got back on track, and both found our way." She squeezed me tighter.

"Do you know where my sister is now? I think of her all the time." I was apprehensive about asking.

"Last I heard, the Mohans moved to North Carolina. They opened their grocery store chain up there, but I didn't keep up with them, obviously." I could tell she didn't like me asking that, so I let it go.

I just hung my head, wondering how hearing all this was supposed to help me heal. I succumbed to my mom's affection, laid my head on her shoulder, and covered my face. The tears just wouldn't stop, and I had no idea why. I didn't know if I was crying for her, my father, or for that little girl sitting in the closet. Either way, this was my last cry over it. I got all the answers I could possibly get. I planned on enjoying this visit with my mom, loving her, and just finally learning to be okay with my life. One thing I did hold in my heart was that I may have been conceived out of love and was meant to be here.

CHAPTER 16

Restored

About two weeks had gone by and no word from Karl. I tried to reach out only twice, but my pride wouldn't let me do too much more. He literally came to my home, fucked me to assert his control, and ghosted me. I was a fool and let it happen. At this point, I really didn't care about what happened at that stupid event or if he was still seeing her. He took me, not her, so this was really her problem or their problem. I just needed to remove myself from this situation; enough of being the jump-off chick.

I had to wonder if I was feeling guilty about letting Mike in that same night, even if nothing happened. Was I just as bad as I thought Karl was? I didn't know. But what I did know was, it was time to start over with working on myself. As for Mike, there was no attempt to contact me, and I didn't try to contact him either. I expected that and was kind of relieved but sad at the same time. Our bond was risky to say the least. If I was supposed to be with him, he wouldn't have been married. Even though he made me feel wanted and good, it wasn't right and eventually I would've been left alone. He married her, not willing to give her up, hint his heart was with her. I was okay with that too.

At work I stayed busy, occasionally visited Francine, and spent a lot of time talking and laughing with Daniel. I knew some of the employees were gossiping, but I paid them no mind. When Karl's sister visited, I would go to my office, knowing Karl probably wasn't too far behind. I avoided that family as much as possible. Francine wasn't happy and said we both were "silly as hell, like high schoolers!" She looked disgusted every time I avoided the Karl conversations.

When I wasn't working, I chatted on the phone with Johnathon, hung out with Mikayla, and I started going to the gym. I ran into Roy a few times when he was playing basketball but remained focused on myself. There was no heavy feeling that I unknowingly had before. Normally, I would've easily given in to Roy's offers of lunch, dinner, or just his addictive, mind-blowing sex, but I didn't want to go there either. Showing myself love, not relying on anyone else was proving to be the key to happiness.

My mind was clear. The conversations with my mom helped me see why I was always so unsure, and why I leaned on men, sex, and unhealthy attention to get by.

She laughed and said, "Well, some of that shit is genetic. What can I say, the Roberts' women have a weakness for men. Just don't let it rule your life like your grandmother and I did. Harness those emotions and see your relationships for what they really are. If it's just sex, know that's all it is. If it's a friendship, know that friends won't hurt you or expect something more from you. But if it's love, take it and hold it, and learn from it. If it doesn't work out, well that person wasn't the one, but you did experience that feeling." Her advice on loving and letting go was priceless.

I couldn't believe she had so much insight into what I was going through. She said counseling while she was in jail helped her. It was kind of a blessing in disguise for her because she couldn't run or self-sabotage.

That visit did so much for me. No nightmares so far, no crying, and my weekends were alcohol free. Sunday was my calm day. I shut the world out by keeping my curtains closed and just watching television. Little did I know, one Sunday my past and stupid decisions would come to haunt me.

That day there was a knock at my door. I opened it to see a short, brown-skinned beautiful woman standing there. *She must have the wrong door*, I figured. She glared at me as confusion settled in my face.

"So, what's your name?" She asked.

"What?" I said, hoping this wasn't what I thought.

"Well, I know you have a name. I'm sure my husband calls you something."

My heart sped up and felt like an impending panic attack. I tried to play it cool. "Your husband? Who's your husband?"

"Mike is my husband. So, what's your name?"

"I'm Lee…umm.. Leesha," I stammered.

"Leesha, how long you been sleeping with him?"

"What? Mike and I were just friends; I haven't seen him in weeks."

"Don't insult me please, Mike has already done enough of that." She crossed her arms, desperately trying to maintain her anger but it was quickly turning into sadness. "I just wanted to see you and wanted you to see me. You need to know that I am a real person, a real woman with real feelings, not just some woman that you have to imagine and can't put a face to. You should know who you are hurting." She teared up. "I don't understand why he is willing to risk his marriage, and you're willing to help him. I don't have any real issues with you, but I'm angry at you too." She wiped the tears away and glared at me again. "Just stop seeing him. Yes, he is the one who should be hearing this, but it's hard to talk to someone's back as they walk away all the time."

"Mike loves you." Okay, I sounded stupid, but I didn't know what to say. Her sadness was becoming mine. I felt so bad for her, but I was the one that caused all this. I just wanted to hug her and apologize a million times, apologize until her heart stopped breaking. But that was impossible.

"If he loves me, then why am I here? Why am I talking to his mistress?" Her voice was shaky.

"Mike and I do not talk any more, we are not together." I began to lose all my energy and leaned back, allowing the door to hold me up. I just wanted to pass out. I owed her answers, but was too cowardly to give them, or just didn't want to cause any more pain. Truth is, if Mike was still having an affair, it wasn't with me; he must have found another woman. I wouldn't dare tell her that.

"It's not what you think, I didn't intend to hurt anyone. I'm sorry, I'm so sorry." I buried my face in my hands. Then I quickly looked up, thinking I should stay on guard just in case she decided to smack me.

"He should be sorry." Her voice was low. She turned and started to walk away.

"I want you to know something too," I called after her. She stopped, didn't turn around, but braced herself, waiting to hear me. "I'm not a bad person, I just made a bad decision, just did a bad thing, and I am sorry my decision caused you so much pain." I was pleading for forgiveness, but I didn't know why. She just walked away.

I went into my apartment and sat on the couch in a daze. I couldn't believe what just happened. That tiny lady made me feel so small. This was all my fault; I should never have entertained him.

I picked up the phone and dialed my mother's number. I burst into tears as soon as she answered. I felt so bad, and angry at Mike and his wife.

"What is wrong with you? Stop crying and tell me."

"I was doing so good, and this guy I was messing with a while ago, it wasn't serious, but his wife came here. I didn't know what to say."

"His wife! What were you doing with him? You know what, never mind. You are not seeing him anymore, right?"

"Yes, I stopped seeing him, but I didn't plan on even seeing him more than once, maybe twice."

"Leesha. Stop it. It's done, it's done." Her voice got calm. "You live and you learn, that's all. Pull yourself together. That lady that confronted you has it way worse than you do, and frankly you didn't help whatever the hell it is they have going on. It's okay to cry and to be upset, but you need to really think about why you are crying. Cause your feelings are hurt? Cause you know it's really over between you and this man; or is it because you two got caught?"

"No! It's because I am sorry and hurting her was never my intention. I haven't seen him in weeks."

"Oh daughter, that was indeed your intention. You were sleeping with a married man, of course you knew you were hurting her. But it's over, so don't let this shake you too much. You were doing good, you were happy. Continue with your journey. A friend once told me, if it won't matter a year from now, don't worry about it too much today."

"You're right. I need to shake this off."

"Good. Now, do tell; what was so great about this man? Details please." Her attempt to lighten the conversation was successful.

"Where do I begin? He was fine, too damn smooth, and a great lover. But now since I met his wife, he's not so sexy anymore."

"Girl! I bet I could've bought you for a nickel when that lady got in your face!" she hollered, then laughed.

"Yes! Bought me for a damn penny, really!" My mother could bring all the country out of me. "I was so damn shocked, I kind of knew it would happen one day when we were seeing each other, but I thought I dodged that bullet when we stopped. My past always comes back to haunt me! Shit!"

"Yea, isn't that the truth." The playfulness was leaving her voice. "You are tough. My advice in this situation is don't speak of it anymore. I mean don't even call and tell him what happened; I'm sure his wife has that covered. If you say something to him, all it would do is start a bigger fight between them, just because you two will look like you're still talking."

"Yeah, that's true, I'm done with that shit." I couldn't agree more.

We chatted for a little longer. I felt better after our conversation. My first instinct was to call her, not Johnathon, which surprised me.

By that evening, the urge to talk to Mike was there. I fought it by going to bed super early but dreamed of Karl. My heart was starting to ache for him again.

CHAPTER 17

Opportunity Knocks

Monday morning, Mr. Bryan, the owner of the facility, stopped by the office. Daniel and I were caught off guard because we were in the middle of our first coffee break. Daniel decided to go do rounds and hurried out.

"Ms. Roberts, can I speak to you for a moment please."

"Yes sir, have a seat please."

"I have great news and it would be better with your help. We love the way this facility is managed. I know my son, Mark, does not give you the support you need, but you do an awesome job. Staff and residents are happy, and this place is maintained well."

"Thank you so much. I really care about the staff and residents and want this to be a good place to work. Also, I like to make sure there is a good work and life balance for all employees, so scheduling is huge." I was about my business when I spoke to this man.

"I know you have been commenting on ways to improve this building. I have an offer for you. We are opening a new facility across town. We have the builder and architect already selected. Plans are almost complete, but I realized we are not the ones that will be working in the new place. We need you as a nurse and an administrator to help make this place not only beautiful but functional and safe."

"I would love to be a part of this! Thank you for thinking of me. Where do I start?"

"Here are the plans." He handed me a stack of papers. "I will email you a link which provides a 3-D tour of how everything is supposed to look. Remember your focus is safety and functionality."

"Ok, I will review all this and provide you with feedback as soon as possible."

"Actually, we will be having a meeting next Monday afternoon. That is the soonest I can get everyone in one room. I will send you a calendar invite with the details. Be prepared to present your wish list. It will be difficult to get buy-in, so be ready for some constructive criticism. They are a tough crowd."

"I will be ready, sir. Thank you for the opportunity."

"See you later." Mr. Bryan walked out.

I was nervous but excited about the opportunity to present my ideas and apply everything I learned in school. I looked through the plans for a while. They were as clear as mud. I checked my email and found the link sent by Mr. Bryan. The 3-D representation of the new facility was beautiful. I noticed it wasn't too far from a major highway. I got my notepad, jotted down designer fence, and looked for examples that wouldn't take away from the beauty of the facility. I had my work cut out for me; these people hadn't even thought about the residents that eloped. I was even more interested in doing this project now.

I spent the next few days walking the hallways, talking to staff, residents, and assessing both the skilled and independent living rooms. I also created workflow diagrams for the nurses, CNAs, housekeeping, and dietary roles, and identified delays and how we could improve just by changing the structure of the facility. I was smart enough to know that this meeting could be the one that determined where the money would go, and representing the staff well was important. By the end of the week, I emailed Mr. Bryan and let him know that I would need an hour for my presentation to include time for questions.

Monday came fast. I spent all weekend working on my presentation. The meeting was at Mr. Bryan's office in the downtown area. I left the facility early to ensure parking, and to have time to freshen up before the meeting. My navy-blue pantsuit, with a cream blouse and heels was accented with pearl earrings and necklace. My hair was pulled back into a neat bun.

I was sitting in the conference room when the planning team started to filter in. My boss, Mark, arrived. He didn't appear to be happy seeing me there. Three other gentlemen came in and sat down, but they didn't acknowledge me. Soon, others walked in and kindly greeted all of us. I was getting more nervous by the minute. To my surprise, Karl walked in. He glanced around the table and his eyes stopped on me. I looked down and started going through my presentation. Butterflies ran wild in my stomach and my whole body became warm.

Mr. Bryan started the meeting. "Good afternoon. I am very excited about today. Most of you know each other, but let's go around the table and do some quick introductions."

I was sitting next to him, so I went first. "Good afternoon, I am Leesha Roberts, administrator of the northside facility, Lotus Gardens. I am here to provide insight on staff workflow and what can be done in this new facility to provide care in a safer more functional way." All the men nodded a hello to me.

"Happy to have you on the team, Ms. Roberts." Mr. Bryan formally welcomed me.

All the other team members quickly introduced themselves. Karl was last.

"I'm Karl Michaels, CEO of KM Construction. Our company oversees the construction aspect. This is a new endeavor for us, because we are known for building homes, but I am happy to say we have all the correct people in place and looking forward to a successful project."

Everyone did a quick overview of their part, and I went right before the finance guys. I guess Mr. Bryan knew my suggestions would require a considerable part of the budget. I requested items such as a designer fence around the facility, extra handwashing stations, hideaway trash bins in the hallways, bigger drains in the showers, and gardens with several sitting areas to improve mental health for the residents. There were several other suggestions, but all came with an in-depth explanation of how it would improve care and the work environment. I got a lot of positive feedback.

"I say we give Ms. Roberts whatever she requests," the financial consultant chimed in.

"Agreed," Mr. Bryant concurred.

I was proud of myself when I left the meeting. Karl had jumped up and rushed out, so I didn't even get a chance to say goodbye. Oh well, that was proof we were done for real.

I called Mikayla to see if she wanted to celebrate with me that evening, but she was busy; then called Johnathon and told him the good news. He sounded tired but was happy for me. I went home and decided to make me some fried fish, red beans, rice, and margaritas for dinner. My cooking was a mixture of my Bahamian and Creole roots now with a San Antonio flair. The beans were simmering with onions, bell peppers, and sausage; the rice was almost done too. My fish had been marinating in lime, salt, various other seasonings, and spices. I was getting ready to coat it in the cornmeal and flour mixture when the doorbell rang loudly over DMX's *Ruff Ryder's Anthem* that was blasting. I took a sip of my margarita and ran to open it. My heart fell to my stomach when I saw Karl standing there.

"Oh, h-h-hello," I stuttered.

"Hey, Lee. Is this a bad time?"

"No, of course not. Come in." I opened the door wider, allowing him in. "I haven't heard from you in a while. What brings you by?"

"I was surprised to see you today. That really fucked me up." He was getting straight to the point.

"It fucked me up too. We ended on uncertain terms, didn't we? You ghosted me, so whatever." I was trying to sound like I didn't even care. "But you got what you wanted, and I didn't expect much more." I was lowkey becoming angry.

"Lee, you know better than that. I was hurt too. You aren't the only one afraid of getting your heart broken. I needed time, and thought I was getting over you, but when I saw you, I knew I wasn't."

"Karl, I will say this one more time. I didn't sleep with that guy; he was just a friend coming to check on me."

"Lee, and one last time, Gina is my ex, she is a drama queen, and she knew what she was doing that night. Nothing was or is going on with us." He was stern.

"I guess we can choose to believe each other or not." I wanted this back-and-forth shit to be over.

"Or we can let this stupidity keep us apart. I'm hoping not." Karl moved closer to me, but I wasn't about to get bedded and left again.

"Would you like to stay for my celebration dinner? I'm making fish with beans and rice, with margaritas." I redirected the conversation.

"Sounds awesome, I'll stay, of course," he agreed.

I secretly hoped that was our opportunity to start over. I did miss him.

CHAPTER 18

All About Karl

That night with Karl started off awkward. I was hesitant to get close to him, but he wasn't. He had seen Mike leaving my place that one morning and now I felt like I was the one that ruined things for us. But I still had a little more growing to do and there was a good reason we had stayed apart.

"You did a good job in the meeting today. Everyone was very impressed with you," he said.

"Thank you, I kind of feel like I over prepared."

"You were very prepared." He laughed. "You looked beautiful, and I couldn't keep my eyes off you."

"Really! I was trying not to stare at you," I admitted.

He looked at me intensely. "I missed you. All I did was wonder what could've been with us, but things got crazy, so fast."

"I know, things did get crazy. I'm sorry about that, but the time apart was good for me," I confessed.

"Good for you, but stressful for me." He was leaning in to kiss me. I had been waiting for that. His kiss was eager, but soft.

I gently pushed him back; he had a confused look on his face. "I don't want to repeat what happened last time we were together," I said.

"What? I don't recall you having a bad time."

"Yeah, but I don't recall you answering my calls or calling me either. So, I'm not just a fuck buddy." I was feeling a little angry.

"Fuck buddy, really? I'm sorry I didn't call, but I was still hurt about you leaving and that guy, but I still wanted you too, it was so confusing."

"Well, you're confused, and me sleeping with you won't help. I'm better than that."

"I know you are. Okay, I'll keep my hands to myself."

"Thank you." I was impressed with my self-control.

Karl and I ended up talking about the new residential facility project and how I got in on it. He was impressed with my in-depth knowledge of how the design would impact the staff's ability to care for the residents. I wanted to include design features that would help encourage care in a holistic way, mind, body, and spirit. Karl watched me intently as I excitedly talked about my ideas and what inspired them.

"You are more perfect than I thought, so beautiful, so smart...so made for me." Karl was looking at the floor when he spoke, almost like he was talking to himself. He finally lifted his head and made eye contact. For the first time I didn't feel the need to avoid his gaze.

"Leesha, I know I deserve to be pushed away because I ghosted you. I was angry and made a mistake. But my real mistake was not letting you know that I wanted you to be mine. I wanted to be exclusive with you. Not talking, dating, or just fucking, but commitment. I just need to know if you want the same because this whole situation is making me sick. I haven't slept well; all I think about is you. I need to know where I stand."

I had never ever had a man say this to me. I was used to men wanting me and keeping his options open, no commitment. Karl wanted to be my man and that was scary. It was time to be honest.

"Karl, you are constantly on my mind too. You're right, we didn't define our relationship when we both knew we wanted more. So, we made a mess. I don't wanna make any more messes, especially with you. You stand here, in my heart and I want to be with you too."

Karl looked relieved. He leaned over and gave me the gentlest kiss. I reciprocated. He was so warm and comforting. His hands traveled, caressing every curve of my body.

"You want me to stop?" he asked.

"No."

"Can we go to your room?" he whispered in my ear.

"Yes."

When we got to the room, he took his shirt off, then removed mine. He laid me down on the bed and finished undressing himself as I took off the rest of my clothes. He kneeled down and kissed my thighs, then gave my pussy a couple of licks, then his lips and tongue softly dominated my breasts. He entered me as he kissed my lips. I gasped as my mind and body surrendered to him. He lifted my legs and slowly made love to me. I felt as if my body was floating. I had never felt such gentleness and passion. Everything he did to me was done with care that I wasn't accustomed to. He stroked me until we both came. That was the first time Karl and I had really made love. We drifted off to sleep for a few hours. I woke up with Karl holding me and felt so wanted, so loved. Karl woke up and squeezed me tighter.

"I missed you so much. We wasted too much time, just being stubborn," he said.

"I needed that time. But it feels so good to have you here. I'm so happy now." That was a new feeling for me. Emptiness was what I usually felt by now with other men, but Karl was different and special.

Later that night, we showered together, ate more food, and talked. We talked about work, future plans, and family. I talked about how important my mother was to me, and surprised myself and told him of my childhood and how my father died. I expected him to shut the conversation down after hearing that drama, but he didn't.

He had a lot to say about his childhood. He told me how Francine and his father's alcoholism impacted their family. His father was found dead in a hotel. There were signs of alcohol and drug use, but Karl was never told exactly what happened. After he died, his mother stayed with Francine and his grandfather. Francine had been a heavy drinker as long as he could remember. I was surprised to hear of the many incidences she was caught in compromising positions by his grandfather. He said she was never really happy in the marriage but was well taken care of by her late husband. He was devoted to her until his death. Karl thought her true love was a man from down the street she was always accused of seeing when his father was a child. He said she never denied or confirmed it. She simply said nothing when confronted with the matter. Karl said his grandfather really died of a broken heart.

According to his memory, she had no remorse, regrets, or anything else that would've hinted toward her love for him. Even though she was a cold-hearted bitch, he loved her and would care for her until her last days. Interestingly, he said it was like she had a spell over people and made them excuse all her sins and heartache that she caused. She was always forgiven and acted as if forgiveness was owed to her by everyone. That wasn't the Francine I had grown to love, but I had seen a bit of her true colors on occasion.

We made love again. I was in control that time. When I slid on top, his eyes sparkled, but he also looked a little nervous. I remembered, a woman like me was new to him. I started off slow and rhythmic. He took a deep breath and shut his eyes tightly. His grip on my hips tightened as if he was trying to control me, but I didn't let him; I moved his hands further down my thighs to take away any control he had on my body. His dick throbbed as I slid up and down. He moaned and set up pulling me into him. Our bodies rocked together until we finished.

It was late and we both had to work the next day. Karl ended up leaving after midnight. I felt so happy and hopeful when he left, almost giddy. I laid in bed thinking about how I missed the conversations with Karl and how I overreacted that night. I should of just kindly took my man's arm and led him away. But no, I was too busy being in my own head with insecurities.

Falling for Karl again was scary for me. I told myself I could handle this; good or bad outcome, I could handle it.

CHAPTER 19

Francine Explained

The next day, Daniel called in sick, so I was solo in the office. Mr. Bryan had called me earlier to let me know how great I did, and I thanked him for the opportunity again. I took a moment to call Johnathon and update him on me and Karl.

"Hey Johnathon!"

"Lee! What's been going on?"

"I have so much to tell you. First, Karl and I are back together. We were together last night after my presentation and made it official."

"Wow, you do have a lot of shit going on. Do tell!"

I told Johnathon about work and Karl. "See, I told you everything would fall into place."

"You were right. Everything has worked out so good it's almost scary. Anyway, what about you? How are you doing?" Johnathon hadn't said much about himself.

"I am doing okay, just taking it easy and hanging with the family."

"Really, nothing exciting going on?"

"No, just resting, sitting on the patio and enjoying life."

"Ok, sounds like you are taking it a little too easy. I want to see you soon. We can chill on the patio together."

"You don't worry about spending time with me. Use your time enjoying Karl and living your best life. You got a lot of life to live, so worry about doing your thing. I have to let you go. We'll talk later."

"Okay, Johnathon. I love you friend, goodbye."

"Love you more, goodbye." Johnathon sounded kind of sad. Maybe his life was just getting too boring. I promised myself I would visit him soon.

I thought of that conversation with Karl about Francine. Things were never as they seemed, and I was beyond curious to hear Francine's rendition of the stories told about her. I decided to make a dinner date with her.

The next evening, I arrived at her place a little earlier than the agreed time. When she opened the door, she seemed surprised.

"I told you I was bringing you dinner." I held up a container of chicken and dumplings, an order of fried fish, and hushpuppies from Acadiana Cajun Café she had requested.

"Oh yes. I almost forgot. Come in, dear." She looked happy, had her make-up on, and hair down.

When I walked in, I was shocked to see Mr. Alberts, one of our longtime residents, sitting on the couch. He jumped up quickly and walked toward the door.

"Francie, I should go. It was nice chatting with you."

"Mr. Alberts don't leave on my account. I can leave the food and we can reschedule, Francie," I teased.

"Very funny, Ms. Roberts. I will see you later, William. Thank you for the kind visit." Her smile was genuine.

"Goodbye ladies." He squeezed past us to get to the door. He smelled nice and his pale blue dress shirt was a perfect contrast to his extra dark, smooth beautiful skin. He was a very handsome older gentleman with a beautiful smile. All the ladies in the facility flirted with him shamelessly. Well, it looked like Francine snagged him.

She shut the door behind him and hurried to her coffee table. There was a book, a decorated box, and several pictures on the table. She hastily threw the pictures in the box.

"Take the food to the dining table and I will open some wine," she said.

"I see you and Mr. Alberts are becoming fast friends."

"Yes, he is a gentleman. But let's have some girl talk. How are you and Karl doing?" She obviously wanted to avoid that conversation.

"We are okay now; taking it slow."

"You see, I told you. You two were made for each other." She laughed.

I could tell that we were going to have a nice time because she was in a great mood. That evening she told funny stories about her kids and how their teachers would call. I gave her a summary about my childhood, and she looked sad as she listened. Then I asked a few questions that cued her in on my conversation with Karl. I didn't want to bring up Karl's father, but it was almost impossible with the direction the conversation was going.

"Yes, my son, Karl's father was an alcoholic. Sorry to say, my husband and I probably caused it." She was tearful but worked hard to keep her composure. "My husband wasn't very nice to me, but he was a doll to everyone else. He was an undercover abusive psycho. Everyone thought he was so nice, so wonderful. Matter of fact, when people were around, I took the opportunity to act like a bitch to him because he wouldn't react in front of them. So, there you have it, my reputation as the biggest bitch that ever walked the earth. No one knew my pain. No one knew how he beat me till I miscarried one of my babies." She began to cry but quickly found her composure again. "My children were taught to hate me and when they got older, they didn't have the sense to see what had really happened. All they know is their father left me everything, and according to them I didn't deserve it. Little do they know, he left me everything out of pure guilt. That was his last fake "I'm sorry." That's why I'm not close to my children. My grandchildren are the ones that care and love me. Karl's mother has always hung around. She calls me 'mother' too. She is probably waiting for me to kick the bucket as well. Thank God my husband died before he could completely poison their minds against me too. I'm sure Karl didn't have too much good to say, but he loves me still. I trust him more than anyone."

"He does love you. Can I ask you a personal question? You don't have to answer if you don't want to."

"Sure, at this age I'm an open book. Someone should know my story."

"Karl said, there were rumors about you having affairs. Particularly with a man that lived down the street when your children were young."

She sighed and the look in her eyes told me this was going to be interesting. I poured us both more wine.

"Did he? I can't imagine what he said. He was nowhere near born. In fact, when those rumors started, my daughter was only ten. That is a very impressionable age for a young girl. My son, Karl's father, was twelve. He was just old enough to understand everything that was being said about me, and I'm sure he was ashamed. But you will be the only one I will tell this story to. At least you will know the truth, I will let all those other assholes' imagination run wild when it comes to me." Her delightfully wicked grin was back. "I surely can't die without anyone knowing what really happened. We lived in a nice well-to-do neighborhood. Everyone was very friendly to each other, except this Black family that lived five houses down. Having Black people pull off buying a house in that neighborhood was very rare, pretty much unheard of. My perception of them was different from the other neighbors, I'm sure. I did make it a point to always wave to them outside and have some small talk when I saw them at the market. I didn't feel one way or the other about them regardless of race. Hell, I was considered white trash when my husband met me. I socialized with everyone, black, white, rich, or poor. They had two girls. Both of them were younger than my children, and the mother was just gorgeous, but frail looking. The father gave new meaning to the words tall, dark, and handsome. Anyway, during that time my husband was abusive to me behind closed doors, and no one knew how miserable and sad I was. He was so mean, and I can easily say I hated him, while everyone loved him. Anyway, one day I noticed that there were several people at that family's home. Everyone was wearing black, hugging and so on. I figured someone had passed. I saw the man walking people in and out. The kids and wife were nowhere in sight. Later, I found out his wife had been sick and passed away. It was so sad, and the poor little girls were surely heart broken." Her look was distant as she spoke. "Anyway, I made a Shepard's pie, baked a pound cake, and took it over a few days later. I knew he worked long hours and would appreciate some food. I did it just to give condolences and help out. We started chatting and eventually formed a friendship. Long story short, yes, we did have an affair. We both were very lonely and sad. Eventually I got pregnant by him. There was no question whose child it was. By that time, I was crazy about him and wanted to leave my husband and have that baby, but I knew that would mean losing my children too. I was confused and scared. My decision was made for me when my husband heard the rumors and realized I was pregnant. He beat me till I lost my baby. I was beyond devastated, and when William found out he wanted to kill my husband. Well, you see how things are now, could you imagine back then, if a Black man killed a white man, after getting his wife pregnant. He would've been dead before he even made it to jail. So, I convinced my husband it was him I loved, and we should move away. I wanted to protect William, but we vowed to keep in touch. That's why I chose to live out the rest of my days here. William is here, my family doesn't know, and I've no intention of telling them."

Her story made me see her in a whole different light. Her life was full of heartache. This was probably why she did and said exactly what she wanted. She was so sad talking about her lost baby and William.

"Wait, is Mr. Alberts your William?" Everything was coming together now. She took a sip of wine, grinned, and winked at me.

That night with Francine was one I will never forget. I hated that she swore me to secrecy. I really wanted to tell Karl and thought it would make him understand her more. I was pretty good at keeping secrets, so I didn't tell.

CHAPTER 20

Johnathon

Karl and I saw each other several times a week and he was a front row witness to my transformation. I loved the time we spent together but didn't let it stop me from working on myself. This time was different from my past episodes of self-improvement. I was my own motivation and wanted this for myself, no one else. I started to look and feel like the woman I dreamed to eventually become.

It had been a month and I continued with my goals of becoming healthier mentally, physically, emotionally, and spiritually. I went to counseling regularly, worked out at the gym three times a week, and cut down on meat and processed foods. My hair was cut in a short sassy style, which was adorned with blond and red highlights. I even learned how to apply eyelashes, got regular massages and facials, and learned how to meditate. I did succumb to medication for depression and anxiety but was okay with that. As a matter of fact, it changed my outlook on everything. I was finally grateful for my life and was happy.

At first, all the "self-love" changes seemed like a chore. It was work going to the gym, work being still to meditate, and work changing my diet. Hell, it was even work flat ironing my hair! Sometimes I thought it was easier being miserable, laying around, having a reason not to improve my life. But honestly, life was moving whether I wanted it to or not, so I may as well be the best version of me. Sometimes when I looked in the mirror, I saw my mother, the poised, unbothered woman coming out on top, regardless of anything. I was going to make it for real this time.

Winter had finally come, which only intensified our romance. Karl started taking me around his friends and more of the extended family. His mother was as cold to me as his sister, but I was unapologetic about seeing Karl. We spent almost every night together. One evening we decided to get cozy at my apartment when my phone rang.

"Hello, is this Leesha?" The voice was vaguely familiar. "This is Stacy, Johnathon's sister."

"Oh hey, Stacy." Why was she calling me and not him? She and I had never been friends. "Is there something going on with Johnathon?"

"Well, he is okay. He is asking to see you and I was hoping you can come down. I know it's short notice, but I think you should come sooner rather than later."

"Johnathon knows I will come see him whenever he wants me to. I'm just wondering why he hasn't asked me himself."

"He didn't want to see anyone. He has been sick, and you know how he is about his appearance." Her laugh was forced.

"Nonsense. Me and him have seen each other at our worst. He's my best friend and you are scaring me right now. What's wrong with him?" I was holding my breath.

This had to be bad. I felt Karl's hand on my shoulder as Stacy's voice turned into a garbled mess like the Charlie Brown teacher. I slipped to the floor when I finally made sense of her words, 'colon cancer and dying.' My world went dark.

My sobs woke me up. When I opened my eyes, confusion almost tricked me into thinking I was having one of my nightmares, but I wasn't. Karl sat down on the bed and tried to comfort me. I looked around the room and saw my small suitcase lying on the floor. There was a pair of jeans and sweatpants hanging over the side.

"Our plane leaves in a couple of hours." He looked at the mess in the suitcase. "I didn't know what to pack for you."

"Arkansas? We are going to see Johnathon, right?" I got out of my bed and assessed Karl's packing skills. Surprisingly, he had most of my regular pieces packed but I threw a few more necessities in. I looked around the room.

"Where's your stuff?"

"I didn't want to leave you. The driver is bringing it when he picks us up. You should eat before we go."

Another surprise, he didn't order out this time. He made hamburgers with potato chips on the side. I felt taken care of, which was foreign but welcomed.

We ate and showered together. Karl held me as the water ran over our bodies, making me feel like everything was going to be okay. I didn't bother straightening my hair, so it was now curled into an afro, another look that Karl hadn't seen. The driver that picked us up was the same one that drove us to the event. He looked a little shocked when he saw me, but quietly drove us to the airport. The car pulled around to an isolated area in the back and there waited a private jet. I was surprised but relieved at our accommodations.

The flight was nice and quiet. My head was clearing up and I was anxious to see Johnathon. Karl had a car waiting for us when we landed, and we went directly to the house.

When we walked in, the house was dimly lit with a stuffy smoke smell. Stacy, two other women, and a man were sitting at a small kitchen table. Our greetings were somber. Stacy took me by the hand and led me to a back room, leaving Karl behind. An older lady in scrubs was sitting just inside the bedroom door. She got up and excused herself when I walked in.

I looked at the bed and all I saw was a thick comforter. Then, Johnathon pulled the blanket down and peered at me.

"You look a fucking mess." His voice was a coarse whisper. "What is going on with your hair?" He tried to smile, but I could tell he was in pain.

"Why didn't you tell me?" Angry tears stung my eyes.

"Tell you what? What was I supposed to say? Hey, I'm dying, and have you breakdown and be all crazy for months and months. No thank you; besides, I love you too much." His frail hand trembled as he motioned for me to come to him.

"I love you more." I hurried over, grabbed his hand, and kissed it.

"Come lay with me."

I slipped under the comforter behind him. "Look, I'm the big spoon now." I was holding his unusually thin frame.

"Ha, Ha." He humored me. "No, seriously I'm glad you're here. As soon as I saw you all my pain went away."

"If I had known, I would've never left your side. I could've cared for you. I love you so much." I let my tears go as I covered the back of his head with kisses.

"I couldn't tell you. Let's not talk about me being sick. Let's talk about the good times, but only after I get the back story on this hair." He smiled.

"The hair is gym friendly, that's all you need to know." He was still the same Johnathon.

"Well, google *'Fraggle Rock'* when you get a chance." He was able to laugh this time. "Just kidding. You know you're gorgeous, I'm just being a hater now. I missed looking at you." His light brown eyes searched my face. "Let's talk about the good times we had together."

"Where should we start? There are so many." I held him tighter.

We talked all night, dozing off and waking up several times. We reminisced about everything from the day we met to the day he left town. He was happy that I was with Karl, and said he was the one for me. Johnathon knew I was being taken care of now, and that gave him some peace. He told me how much he loved me and if he hadn't gotten sick, he would've happily married me because our past relationships sucked so badly. That was funny, but I knew it was true. At one time, I would've said the same thing because what would've had been better than marrying my best friend? But this was happening. My best friend was on hospice and dying before my eyes. Nothing could've prepared me for that.

The sun was beaming through a small crack in the curtain when I woke up. I looked by the door and there was no hospice nurse. Johnathon's body was in my arms, but he wasn't there. I cried as I rocked him back and forth. There was a light knock at the door and Stacy peeked in.

"Is he…gone?" Her voice was shaky, then she just wailed.

I jumped up and gave her the tightest hug I could. She leaned on me for support. There were no words to comfort her.

"Thank you for coming. Johnathon said he wanted to be next to you when he took his last breath." Finally, she was able to speak.

That hit me like a ton of bricks. How could I go on now? This forever changed my life for the worse.

The older lady came rushing in straight to the bed and held him.

"My baby, my baby!" Her cries ripped the soul out of me. There wasn't anything like a mother's cry for the loss of a child.

I left the room, leaving Stacy and her mother alone. Karl was sitting up on the couch. He looked disheveled. I realized he had slept there. He got up and gave me a hug.

"I'm sorry about your friend," he whispered.

"Thank you for bringing me. I'm sorry I fell asleep. I thought you would've gotten a hotel."

"No, I wasn't going to leave you, that's what I'm here for."

"Thank you so much," I spoke calmly but the tears wouldn't stop.

The nurse made a call and was now in the bedroom. Everything was so surreal. I couldn't believe what had just happened. For me, it was so quick. I had no time to process this, prepare for this, or be okay with this. It wasn't fair, but I knew this was how Johnathon wanted things to be. It comforted me to know that it was me he wanted to spend his last moments with. This was tough.

Karl and I spent the rest of the day at a hotel. We ordered room service and prepared for the flight home the next day. Johnathon's sister treated me like family. She called me a few times, discussing his final wishes. She actually laughed when she told me he was going to be in black and red and said I must do the same. Typical Johnathon, dressing me up even in death.

The next morning, we ate breakfast, packed up, and caught the jet back. Karl was making this nightmare bearable. I didn't know how I could've made it through without him. The funeral was going to be next week. I took off for the rest of the week just to get my mind together and prepare for the worst day of my life. I stayed at Karl's place most of the time, and that was helpful. He didn't leave my side, and all he wanted to do was make sure I was okay. Had this happened eight months ago, there was no way I could've survived this. But I was grateful for God's timing if this had to happen. It's almost like Johnathon waited until I was strong enough to endure this, and for someone to love me through it.

Thursday came, and once again, Karl and I were boarding his private jet. When we arrived in Arkansas, our first stop was Johnathon's house. More family members gathered there, and they were very welcoming. Everyone knew me and Karl by name. We stayed there for a few hours then went to our hotel to prepare for the service the next day.

Karl wore all-black, and I had a black, midi skirt with a matching jacket and a black dressy hat that tilted to the side. It was accented with a bright red handkerchief, and a small dark blue ribbon for colon cancer awareness. I had my bright red lipstick and nail polish on. Surely Johnathon would approve of this look.

The church was huge with exquisite cement detail in the front. The ceiling was high, and the windows were stained with depictions from the bible. It was so packed. As soon as we got there, a short man I recognized from the day before, came and rushed Karl and me to a back room where the family was gathered. There, we all held hands and said a prayer. As Karl squeezed my hand, I felt a warmness engulf me. It felt like one of Johnathon's comforting hugs.

"I can't do this," I said to myself as my tears fell.

"Yes, you can," someone whispered in my ear, but no one was right there. That small voice that I only heard gave me a little strength. We all walked down the long aisle together. Karl and I ended up sitting at the end of the third pew. There was a pearl white coffin adorned in red roses. The front of the church was an ocean of red and white roses. The packed pews were an indicator of the love that surrounded Johnathon. I thought back to all the times he said he moved because he was so alone, no one loved him, and he had no one. Well, from the looks of it, he had many people in his life. But I also knew "friends and family" came out of the wood works when someone died.

The short man, that I learned was his cousin, was the officiant. The choir did a few songs and then there was a call for remarks. I wanted to say something, but my grief wouldn't let me. Several people had touching stories. Finally, the remarks were ending, and Johnathon's cousin looked my way.

"Now, I'd like to invite Ms. Leesha Roberts to speak. She was Johnathon's best friend."

I was surprised because I didn't commit to making any remarks. I figured it would be too hard for me to do. Karl looked at me, his eyes asking if I was okay. I nodded. The next thing I remember was standing in front. I didn't even remember the walk up there; it was almost like I blacked out for a few seconds.

I looked over the crowd, thankful half my face was covered by my hat and took a deep breath to steady myself.

"First, my condolences to Johnathon's family. Over the last few days, I have seen where all of his caring and loving ways came from. Thank you for welcoming me in this very difficult time. Like Pastor Allen said, Johnathon was my best friend, and I can truly say I loved him more than I ever thought I could love anyone." Tears clouded my eyes. "He spent countless nights lending me his shoulder to cry on or listening to my problems; those problems now seem very small. I am glad he is no longer hurting but he has left a void that is impossible to fill. I could talk forever about how important he was to me, and about all of the good times we had. I still can't bear the thought of spending one day without him, and my mind still cannot accept that he is gone." I looked at the casket and my heart ached and said my last words to him.

"Johnathon, I want you to know that I feel you every moment of my life. You are in my heart, and I will always hold on to you. I will reluctantly carry on, but I anxiously wait for the day I can hold you again." My tears were uncontrollable as I walked back to my seat.

Karl gave me a hug when I sat down. For a second, I wished for his arms to be Johnathon's, but was grateful for his presence. He did everything he could to get me through this, but he couldn't do anything about the immense grief I was feeling. Some days, I tried to hold it together, trying to give him a break from the emotional roller coaster he was on with me. I couldn't even get through a meal without crying. But that day was final and marked the end of a chapter that was supposed to continue forever. That day forced me to carry on without my best friend.

CHAPTER 21

The Past has Arrived

Weeks after the funeral, I was feeling almost like myself again. Karl was back traveling for work, and I was back working, visiting Francine, and having morning coffee with Daniel. I was down a few more pounds and had gotten used to the short hair. I was doing well and planned to take Karl to visit my mother and James in a few weeks.

It was Wednesday evening, and Karl was coming over on his way from the airport. He claimed he couldn't wait any longer to see me. I cooked steak, potatoes, and green beans. The house was deep cleaned, and candles were lit. My outfit was simple with an off the shoulder shirt and white shorts. I always wonder why he enjoyed coming to my house instead of his beautiful home. I still got nervous and excited when I saw him. That was a good thing.

When I opened the door, he scooped me up and kissed me.

"I missed you so much."

"You were only gone four days. I cooked for you." I was playfully pushing him away.

"Okay, thanks. We can eat later, or you can eat later." He picked me up, and I laughed as he carried me to the bedroom.

Karl laid me on the bed kissing me, and I tried not to act like a giddy teenager, but this man made me so happy. He took my shirt off and unsnapped my bra, letting my breasts fall. He backed off for a moment and admired me then he kissed me again. He moaned, "I love you, Lee." I stopped breathing for a second and looked into his eyes.

"You do? You're not playing with me, are you?" I knew that was coming but was still surprised.

"Yes, I do, I'm not playing. I can't stop thinking of you when we are apart. I always want to make sure you're good because I just love you so much."

I had never heard a man say those words to me. I looked at him and thought for a second, then said, "I love you too, Karl."

A warm feeling rushed through my body as he leaned in to finish what he had started. He kissed me, then my breasts, giving me light licks in between. He was such a passionate man. His tongue traced down my stomach slowly and his hands grasped my soft hips as they were liberated from my shorts. His fingers pulled my lace panties to the side and rubbed my pussy. He pulled them off and slowly licked my center, then came up kissing and sucking my breasts again. I exhaled, allowing him to enter and gently make love to me. Karl was so intoxicating.

Later that night, I was awake, looking at him as he slept. *Is this what true love feels like?* There was no worry about him running home to his wife or adding me to a harem of women. For the first time in my life, I wasn't just a pretty face with a pussy. He took care of me through the worst time of my life, slept with me every night, and didn't expect anything from me. His only goal was to make sure I slept, ate, and not drown in my tears.

I felt so fragile, and he made sure I didn't break. But the hard work, self-love and commitment to holistic self-care had also paid off. Being in a good place emotionally to handle this made all the difference in the world. Finally, my heart was capable of completely loving myself and loving someone else too. Karl was the one and there was no fear of commitment or loneliness. I was in the perfect space for what was about to happen next.

We were in a deep sleep when my phone rang. It was an unknown number that had called me several times. This time I picked it up, hoping to opt out of what I thought was a telemarketer call. Whoever this person or company was, they were a pain in my ass.

"Hello!"

"Good morning. May I speak to a Leesha Reneé Roberts?" *Who in the hell is using my whole name?*

"This is Leesha." I was curious now.

"Finally, I got a hold of you. I can say this was going to be my last time calling for you."

"What can I help you with, sir?"

"Yes, my name is Rodney Tanner, and I am Elizabeth Mohan's lawyer."

"Okay." I didn't recall the name Elizabeth.

"I regret to inform you that Mrs. Mohan has passed away. Unfortunately, I'm contacting you late, her service was weeks ago."

"Oh, I am sorry to hear that. My father's name was Lee Mohan, but I do not recall anyone by the name of Elizabeth."

"I figured you would say that. Mrs. Elizabeth Mohan was your grandmother, Lee's mother." My chest was growing tight, and Karl was staring at me by this time.

"Okay, my condolences to the family. Thank you for letting me know." I was ready to end this conversation. I had already missed her funeral, so we were done.

"I am her lawyer and was appointed as the executor of her will. I plan to notify the family of the details Monday morning, and you should do your best to come. Once again, I am sorry for the short notice."

"Sir, I really don't think I need to be there. I haven't spoken to that family since I was a child, and don't want to impose. But thank you for calling me."

"Ms. Roberts, I don't think you understand. You want to be present for this, so Mrs. Mohan's wishes can be carried out appropriately. Please, do you need help getting down here?"

"No, sir, I don't need help. I may not be there but thank you." I didn't know how to handle this; my first instinct was to run from the situation.

"Very well; but let me give you the information in case you change your mind." Mr. Tanner sounded defeated.

He gave me all the information I needed to attend this meeting. I didn't agree to go because I was scared and knew that family didn't want to see me of all people. When I hung up the phone, I told Karl about the conversation and got online to check the price of the flights to North Carolina just for kicks. Apparently, the Mohans had moved from Louisiana to North Carolina several years ago. It was scary to even think about going. *Who would be there?* My mind was getting the best of me now.

"First of all, what are you doing? Why don't you take our private plane? I mean, my plane." I could tell the slip up made him uncomfortable.

"Well, I didn't want to assume I can just jump on your private plane and take off."

"Lee, you are welcome to whatever I have. Anyway, I will make arrangements for you. I don't know if I can go, but maybe we can get your mother here to go with you."

"Well, I don't think so. I'm sure the other attendees will not want to see the woman who killed my father, considering that is his family."

"Okay, I will rearrange my schedule. I don't want you to go alone."

"I'm a big girl, but okay, if you want to go."

Karl worked his magic, and we were set to leave early Monday morning. The meeting was to take place in the late afternoon. I was a ball of nerves waiting. What was this all about? That old lady probably wanted me to know how much she despised me and my mother. Maybe that was all this Mr. Tanner had to say to me.

I called my mother to tell her about Mrs. Mohan. She sounded uneasy about the whole situation.

"Leesha, be careful with those people. I know for sure Mr. Mohan hated me dating your father, Mrs. Mohan just never said anything. She let him do all the ranting."

"I never asked what happened to Helen after my dad died."

"Well, I heard she succumbed to breast cancer seven years ago."

"How come you didn't tell me as soon as you found out?" I asked.

"I don't know, I just didn't want to bring back old memories for you."

"Oh, I would've wanted to know about that. She is my sister's mother." I felt a lump forming in my throat.

"I'm sorry. I should've told you."

"Yes." I couldn't hold back my tears. "Mom, what about my sister? Do you think she will be there?"

"I'm pretty sure she will. Lee, whatever happens and whatever is said, just be strong and think clearly, and know I love you so much." My mom talked like she knew something terrible was going to happen.

"I know, but I can't wait to see my sister, that's the only reason I'm going."

"Okay, Leesha, be strong."

"Mom, I'll talk to you later." I hung up and instantly felt sick. Something was off about that whole conversation.

When Karl and I arrived in North Carolina, we checked into a beautiful historical hotel and had a late lunch at their restaurant. I was getting accustomed to this lifestyle, but still felt a little out of place sometimes. We still turned heads when we walked into any room, but I wasn't sure if it was a good or bad thing.

Mr. Tanner's office was close to our hotel. The waiting room was decorated with heavy dark wood pieces and smelled of lavender. The secretary was a bubbly, flirtatious blond that did everything but fall to her knees for Karl's attention. We sat and waited for God knows who.

The wait was aggravating me, and I was losing my nerve about the possibility of seeing Leanna. I wanted to ask Ms. Blondie if Mr. Tanner could just see me since everyone else was late. Just as I started approaching the front desk, the door swung open and in walked a tall, young woman with dark hair that exaggerated her white porcelain skin. A short, heavy man, and another older woman accompanied them.

The younger woman was carrying a worn wooden box. They looked at me and the shock was evident. I didn't recognize anyone, but that didn't surprise me. Karl got protective immediately, grabbed my arm, and led me back to the chair. He peered at them before he sat down. I got nervous, because this was already an uncomfortable scene; but what in the hell did I expect? I had to remind myself that I was called there and didn't start this mess.

Finally, we were welcomed into a spacious meeting room with a table and chairs in the middle. This room smelled of fresh wood and leather. Mr. Tanner sat down at the head of the table. The other three people sat on the opposite side of me and Karl. We opted to sit close to the door. It surprised me to find out that the porcelain doll was Leanna Mohan when the introductions were made. She looked completely different. Her sweet demeanor was now cold and angry; it kept me from reaching out and hugging her. The older woman was her aunt, and the short man was her uncle. I had my sister, aunt, and uncle sitting across from me. They had never contacted me after my father's death, so I assumed they didn't like me. The older woman broke the silence.

"Rodney, why is this woman here? She never even knew my mother." She spoke like I disgusted her.

"Ma'am." He glanced over his glasses. "Ms. Roberts is here because I am the executor for your mother's will, and I required her to attend. I don't have time to chase everyone, so here you are, together. Besides, she is not 'this woman,' that is your niece. The late Mrs. Mohan thought of her often and considered her as much family as you all are. Now, if you don't mind, I need to get on with this."

He read a list, not the actual will. "Beth, as her daughter, she left you two properties worth approximately 10 million dollars. Thomas, as her son, left you the other two properties worth approximately 8.5 million dollars. Leanna, as her youngest granddaughter, she left you the stable with the horses, worth nine hundred thousand dollars and the vacation homes, worth seven million dollars. Mrs. Mohan leaves one million dollars to multiple charities."

The Mohans seemed disappointed but continued to look at Mr. Tanner intensely.

They sickened me. They were left with millions of dollars in property, and they were disappointed? Was this a fucking cruel joke? What the hell was I here for? I squirmed in my chair and Karl gently touched my leg. He knew I was done with this shit.

Mr. Tanner continued, "Ms. Leesha Renée Roberts, Mrs. Mohan wanted you to know that she thought of you every day since you came into this world. Circumstances kept her away, but in death she wishes you to be taken care of. With that being said, Ms. Roberts, she has allotted you the remainder of her estate, worth 40 million dollars." Mr. Tanner flipped through his papers. "I need some signatures." Karl and I sat there in complete shock.

"Wait a minute!" the older woman yelled. "You can't be serious. These people tore my family apart, killed my brother. I was always by mother's side!"

My sister just sat there with tears streaming down her face in disbelief; or was it the sting of Elizabeth Mohan's betrayal that caused her reaction?

"These are not my wishes; these are your mother's. This Will was written years ago, and it wasn't a sudden decision." Mr. Tanner had a slight look of glee on his face.

Leanna peered at me and finally spoke. "Your mother should still be rotting in prison, but she isn't because my mother helped her." Her voice trembled with anger. "My mother and your mother plotted my father's murder. I heard them talk about it; I just didn't know what I was hearing. What do you think of your abused, innocent mother now, Leesha Renée?"

"Leanna, that was never proven. That is enough! This is not why we are here!" Mr. Tanner was noticeably upset.

"Ask her! Ask your bitch of a mother!" Leanna didn't back down.

"My bitch of a mother? I think you got my mother confused with your evil ass mother." I felt Karl squeeze my leg as if he were begging me not to respond anymore.

"Enough! Let's get to business!" Mr. Tanner wanted it to end, but not as badly as I did. Leanna just sat back in her chair and smirked at me. She knew her words stung.

Finally, I signed the papers and this little Black girl that sat in the closet was now a millionaire.

"Oh, I almost forgot. Leanna, do you have the box?" Mr. Tanner's voice was now nonchalant. She slammed the heavy box on the table in anger. Mr. Tanner flipped through his papers and pulled out a small brown envelope and slid it to me. I picked it up and looked in it, glimpsing at an old key. Now, I was wondering what was next. He began reading again.

"My Little Leesha, I kept diaries throughout most of my life. All my family knows me, except you. I leave you all my diaries so you can truly meet me and know my thoughts, and experiences. You will also discover my deepest secrets, so read and learn my lessons. Maybe you are not interested now, but one day you will be curious."

Mr. Tanner looked at me. "Mrs. Mohan was a very vivacious woman. I wish I could read her diaries." He chuckled.

I was crying now; this was all so much. I had my life turned over in these few minutes.

"Thank you," I whispered.

The Mohans stood up. "We will be getting a lawyer. This is bullshit." They walked out the door.

I couldn't let Leanna leave without me saying something. That little girl had haunted me for years. I had to get something off my chest.

"Leanna," I called out. "You're my sister and I missed you. I'm sorry for not saying goodbye, I'm sorry for not giving you a hug. Everything that happened had nothing to do with us. We were just kids." My voice trembled. "I just need you to know that. I hope one day, things will be different."

Leanna stood there for a second with her hands shaking. Suddenly, she ran up and gave me a tight hug. This was the hug that should have happened the day I left my father's house; her tough demeanor disappeared for just a second, then just as quickly, she turned and left. My aunt and uncle followed behind her. No goodbye or any acknowledgement that I was their family too, and their disregard hurt me. I knew why they felt that way, but I was just a child when everything happened. At least there was a chance for Leanna and me.

"Thank you, Mr. Tanner." I felt the need to thank him one more time.

"You're welcome. Mrs. Mohan wondered about you often. But she was afraid of causing family division by contacting the woman that was responsible for her son's death. Well, you understand." He had a sympathetic look on his face.

"No, I can't say that I do understand, but I accepted it a long time ago." I walked out. Karl grabbed the box and hurried to catch up to me.

The ride back to the hotel was quiet. My mind was racing. Any other time, I would call my mom right away, but it was too much to talk about right now.

"Are you okay? You should be; you're a millionaire now and life has changed." Karl squeezed my hand. "And you are going to get to know the lady that made it happen." He touched the locked wooden box.

"Yes, I know. I'm just ready to get back home, back to normal." I was happy but confused.

The trees raced by, but the car seemed to be motionless. What Leanna said to me ruined my ability to be as happy as I should've been. The more I thought about it, the more I realized what she said about our mothers may be true. I would hate to think of my mom taking part in the premeditated murder of my father, but it was possible. When Mom got out of jail, we moved, got a pretty nice house, and car. I never even wondered where the money came from. Now it was obvious the money came from Helen and my father's estate. I didn't know how to feel because my father was a cruel asshole, but did he deserve to be killed? I had to talk to Mom about this.

Later that night, we ate a nice dinner and drank too much wine. I made a toast to the great Elizabeth Mohan, the woman that changed my entire life with her dying wishes. I was feeling lighter and happier by this time. At least someone from that family thought about me and possibly even loved me. That thought made me realize my assumptions caused me too much pain in this life. Someone else did care about me, so it seems. I was happiest about Leanna's hug and the possibility that we could have a relationship one day.

I called Mom as soon as I got back home, and Karl left. The best thing to do was to just ask and not beat around the bush.

"Hello." She sounded cheerful when she answered the phone.

"Hi, Mom, how are you?"

"I'm okay, just anxious to hear about your trip."

"Well, Elizabeth Mohan was my dad's mother. Apparently, she was pretty well off. Her lawyer called us there to make sure her Will was carried out as she wished."

"Us? Who all was there?"

"Leanna, her aunt, and uncle."

"Wow…"

"Wow is right. Anyway, Ms. Mohan left them land and money, millions."

"Okay. What did they want you there for?"

"They didn't want me there. Her lawyer insisted I come, and they were angry when they saw me. Mr. Tanner shocked the room when he disclosed what the late, great Mrs. Mohan left me. Apparently, she thought of me often and wanted to reach out but was afraid to cause turmoil in the family. She left me her diaries and a lot of money."

"What! How much is a lot? Wait, don't tell me, but is it enough for you to be comfortable?"

"She left me more than enough. But Leanna was so angry, she blurted out that you and her mother planned my father's death. She claims to have heard you two talking about it but was too young to understand what was going on."

"Well, that's…that's crazy. I hope you didn't believe all that."

"Mom, tell me about your and Helen's relationship. Were you friends with her?"

"We talked; we had some things in common obviously. Lee, we both knew your dad was a loose cannon. Think about it. If he never came to my home to attack me, all of that would've never happened."

"Mom, but you knew he would come over, and you knew what you were going to do when it happened, because you planned it?"

"You mean, I planned to defend myself when he showed up to beat my ass. Okay, yes, I did get a gun to protect myself from him."

"Got a gun from where? Who gave you it?"

"Lee, all you need to know is I had a gun and shot your dad. I regret it every damn day of my life, and regret everything from the day we met. The only good thing that came out of us was you. Forgive me for all my stupid mistakes, but premeditated murder, no, not me. I got it to scare him but ended up getting beat so bad and feeling so betrayed and angry, I killed him." There was so much pain in her voice.

"But you could've let him walk away, Mom."

"I know, I was wrong. I hated myself for years, but I had to move on. You need to move on too, because this has no business taking up space in your life. You understand?"

"I guess I have to, I have no choice." I would never know the truth and was unsure how to feel about it, but either way, the past couldn't be changed.

CHAPTER 22

Making the Adjustment

A couple of weeks had gone by, and things were strangely the same. I didn't buy a new car or a house. I didn't quit my job and no one outside of my family and Karl knew what happened. My mother didn't accept any money from me. She insisted that she and James had enough, and they were comfortable. I really think she felt guilty about taking anything from the Mohans.

One thing I did was decide to take some time off and go to Hawaii for two weeks. Karl was disappointed when I told him that I purchased first-class tickets and paid for our resort stay. He claimed that I just had to say I wanted to go, and he would've taken me in a heartbeat. Karl insisted that saving and investing was the way to go. He also informed me that yes, it was a lot of money, but people could blow through it easily if not careful. I just wanted to do this for us.

I bought a new bathing suit for every day we were going to be there, even added some cute sundresses and sexy lingerie. Karl had some pieces to match mine.

Our flight was relaxing, and the smell of hibiscus and plumeria filled the Hawaii airport. When we got to the resort, I was so amazed by the turquoise water. Our suite had floor to ceiling windows, and everything was perfectly placed. The smell of the ocean and fresh flowers was incredible.

After a mini tour, we put on our bathing suits and headed to the beach. We did a little swimming but mainly lounged, drank fruity cocktails, held hands, and talked. I felt so free, and that was going to be an experience I would never forget. Karl's generous tips ensured that our time there would be perfect. We spent the week doing activities, fine dining, and making love.

Our last week was approaching fast. One evening, we went to our favorite restaurant. I felt beautiful in my rose-colored halter dress that opened to the small of my back, revealing my tan lines. Karl opted for dark jeans and a nice, collared shirt. We were eating dessert when the waiter came by with some champagne we didn't order. I told the waiter he had the wrong table when Karl picked up a little black box from the serving tray. I gave him an inquisitive look as the waiter stepped aside.

"I love you more than you could possibly imagine." Karl got on one knee. "You are the person I have been waiting for my whole life. I want to come home to you every day. Lee, will you marry me?"

I thought about all I had been through to get to this point. I really made room for the love of my life. Now here he was, proposing to me.

"Yes, Karl, I will marry you."

My answer was easy because I felt the same way. We hugged and kissed, and the restaurant erupted with people clapping. I was embarrassed and looked at everyone. The dimly lit restaurant now had the lights on. I was stunned to see my mother and James standing up. She blew me a kiss. Then I saw Mikayla and her new man. A couple more tables over, there was Daniel and his wife. Francine, Mr. Alberts, and one of my favorite nurses from the facility sat at Daniel's table. I was a little teary eyed when I looked at Karl. He gave me a smile, grabbed my hand, and we greeted everyone. We danced and drank champagne the rest of the night. I was finally happy.

That night, I dreamed of Johnathon. He was pushing me on a swing and singing. That was weird because he never sang. Then he was in the swing next to me. We held hands as we swung back and forth and he told me that he was the best he'd ever been, and he was happy for me. He looked up in the sky and yelled, "Look!" His finger was pointing at a white bird in a tree, and then the dream was over. The next morning, as I was getting out of bed, I found a small white feather next to my feet. I picked it up and took it as a sign that Johnathon was nearby.

Karl and I spent the remainder of the trip enjoying everyone. I found out that he had paid for all of them to join us. Once again, he surprised me. I'd always been loved by these people, and hated spending so much of my life believing I wasn't worthy of anyone's love. God showed up for me. Now I knew he had always been next to me, even through my mess. I always deserved something and someone great.

EPILOGUE

looked across our backyard at my family and friends. Everyone was there celebrating the twin's second birthday. My beautiful little ladies' names were Lizzie and Frankie, after Elizabeth Mohan and Francine. I had grown to know and love the late Mrs. Mohan from reading her diaries. She was beautifully complicated, dwelled on her flaws, and the bad things that happened in her life consumed her. But she persevered and sacrificed all her dreams for her family. I could relate to her. After seeing pictures, I found she was the woman responsible for my curvy body. Francine, well, she got her namesake simply because she brought me and Karl together.

Lizzie and Frankie were fraternal twins. Lizzie had a darker complexion with dark, wavy hair and lighter eyes. Frankie had a lighter complexion with lighter, tightly coiled hair and darker eyes. They were complete opposites, but both were the cutest little girls. They had Karl wrapped around their fingers. He was like their genie, anything they wanted, he got them. I was the bad guy, and knew he was creating little monsters, but they were his monsters, and that was a losing battle for me.

Our life together was beautiful. We had our wedding right in our backyard. When I saw this house, I had to have it. Karl bought it as a surprise and early wedding gift, so I had the wedding there. That was one day I will never forget. But the birth of the girls was the best day of my life. Now I was waiting for the birth of our son, and Karl was beyond excited.

He came over and gave me a hug. "Can you believe all of this? All from a forced lunch date."

We looked over at Francine, who was indulging in a bit too much alcohol. But that was okay with us because she had her own room at our home and could stay anytime she pleased. Mom, James, and Karl's mother were monopolizing the girls. That was okay too. This was my life, and it had turned out unexpectedly perfect. I remained lost in my thoughts as Karl walked away to greet more guests.

I still wished Leanna could be here, but she wasn't ready to be around my mother yet. As for our relationship, we still had a lot of work to do. We spent time together periodically. I'd been to her home, and she was trying to teach me to ride horses before I got pregnant with the girls. She came to the hospital after they were born late one night and did the auntie thing while Karl went to get rest at home, and I slept. Lizzie and Frankie were premature, so our stay in the hospital was a little longer. She stepped up, bringing me food and rocking the girls. So now we see each other occasionally.

She was busy with school, and I was busy with the girls and running Lotus Gardens still.

Through all of this, signs of my guardian angel comforted me. A white feather flew in my hair during our wedding, and a small white bird was outside my hospital window the night the twins were born. Every time I wished Johnathon was there for a special day, he showed up in his own way. That was what I chose to believe. My thoughts of contentment and gratefulness were quickly interrupted by Karl's voice.

"Hey Lee, I want you to meet our new company lawyer I've been talking about." Karl was right behind me by the time I turned around.

My eyes quickly glanced at the lawyer he had been raving about. I didn't even have to look at his face to know who he was. I knew him by the way he stood and his build. This man had spent several nights in the old Leesha's bed. There stood a clean-shaven Mike. I was having a silent anxiety attack when Mike held out his hand.

"Mrs. Michaels, it's so nice to finally meet you," he smiled.

Something told me, my world was about to spin out of control.

NOTE FROM THE AUTHOR

Thank you for indulging in this journey. My goal in writing this story was to create a relatable protagonist in Leesha, one whose journey would resonate with readers. Though flawed and prone to poor decisions, Leesha grappled with the questions many women face about themselves and while in relationships. Her character illustrates how past experiences often dictate our present and future behavior. Leesha's self-improvement journey was significant and reflected the universal struggle of self-love and acceptance.

I wanted Leesha to serve as a mirror, reflecting both the mistakes we are liable to make and our capacity to learn and grow. Though her choices may sometimes seem frustrating, my aim was to make her human and complex.

What began as a personal, guilty-pleasure writing experience evolved into a labor of love. It is my hope that you connected with Leesha and her journey on an emotional level.

If you enjoyed this book, please help me spread the word by leaving an online review on any of the platforms where the book is sold. Thank you!

~Jennifer Janell

DISCUSSION QUESTIONS

1. What are some of Leesha's characteristics you can relate to, good or bad?
2. Why do you think Johnathon really hid his illness from Leesha?
3. What is one thing you would change about Karl?
4. Do you think Leesha's mother has more secrets to be revealed?
5. In the end, Mike returns. How do you think Leesha will handle his new role in her life?

… Get ready for The Betrayal of Lee.

www.ingramcontent.com/pod-product-compliance
Lightning Source LLC
Chambersburg PA
CBHW021547310726
48972CB00003B/716